MARC JILLSON & THE GAZEBO

Love Inscribed #2

ANYTA SUNDAY

First published in 2020 by Anyta Sunday
Buerogemeinschaft ATP24, Am Treptower Park 24, 12435 Berlin

An Anyta Sunday publication
www.anytasunday.com

ISBN 978-3-947909-22-3

Line Edited by HJS Editing
Proofread by Lynda Lamb @ Refinery

For Sunne, without you this book wouldn't exist.

CONTENT WARNING

References of past homophobic violence, mentions of the
Vietnam War and the draft

CHAPTER ONE

To visit him in jail, or not to visit?

Time was ticking. If I was gonna make it, I needed to leave now.

I should visit. Except . . .

Echoes of long-healed bruises ghosted my undereye and snuck down my arm.

It'd only been nine months since that night. Nine months stewing in past bad decisions. Nine months barely making it to lectures and scraping through exams. Nine months restricting myself to online life.

I shouldn't visit him. Shouldn't dredge all that up.

My foot jiggled a *leave-now, leave-now* rhythm, while my heart beat a scared *or-not, or-not.*

I stuffed Cheetos into my mouth, gripped my console, and moved my knight, Fawkes, through creepy, thick woods.

A familiar mage popped out from behind a tree—tall, muscular, beautiful . . . .

My knight fell on its heavily armored ass.

The chat box lit up and I jumped into the distraction.

DaMage: I figured out who you are, Fawkes.

Me: I'm your best bet at survival.

DaMage: You're Marc Jillson. I can't believe I've been playing all summer with YOU!

I stiffened on my chair.

Me: Do we know each other in real life?

DaMage: *Know* takes it too far. You used to write for the *Scribe*.

Me: How'd you figure it out?

DaMage: I have my genius ways.

Me: Hack my profile?

DaMage: Confession . . . I'm really good at it.

My stomach sickened. He knew the real me?
Definitely shouldn't have baited the mage. He claimed to be 100% Geek Force, and I'd demanded proof. Apparently I'd underestimated his tech savviness.
I ground my knuckles over a long-winded "Fuuuuuuck."
My foot jiggled harder.

Me: What else you got on me?

DaMage: You study history and economics. Prof. Carol's 302. Prof. Velazquez's 311. Prof Shammas' 324. Me too.
My fingers hovered over the keys. *Have we met in person?*

Me: Enough chit-chat. We have demons to slay.

DaMage: That's your problem, Marc. You always claim the need to slay demons, yet you never do.

Me: Ohhhh, game fucking on.

I raced my knight through the woods to the cave of night-mares and charged in—gutsy, sword leading the way. DaMage glided gracefully to my side, a ball of light sparkling in his grip.

Real-life knocking broke my concentration. I swung toward the reverberations shaking the cherry-wood basement door. "Marc. You in there?"

Hinges squealed. I abandoned the console and leaped up. "Uncle Ben. Yeah, I'm here."

My uncle stalled two steps into my bedroom, plate in hand. A muffin with a blazing birthday candle. He stroked his salt-and-pepper beard, dark gaze absorbing the room. Dog-eared books littered the couch. The comforter lay strewn atop unfolded laundry on my desk chair.

He focused on me in my sweatpants and the smudged T-shirt clinging to abs that had almost lost their definition.

"When you said you had plans for your birthday, I didn't think you meant . . . this."

I glanced at the screen; a demon was munching on my soul. Dammit. "I didn't want to put you out. This is great."

"This is sad, Marc." He gestured to the computer screen, where a smartass reply popped into the chat box. "Who's your online friend?"

"Just a dude," I said evasively. "Someone from around here."

"You've met him in real life?"

"Not exactly."

"Video called him? Verified his age?"

"No. What's with the frown?"

"Just don't want you catfished."

"We're both into role-playing. He's a kickass mage and I'm his knight in shining armor." Uncle Ben's expression visibly contorted from information overload.

I blanched. "Role-playing *games*. Fantasy. I mean . . . fuck. Nothing is going on. Nothing."

"I wish there was."

I flushed, hard. "What?"

Uncle Ben waved away my assumption. "Not between you and your role-playing friend. I wish something was happening in your *real* life."

"Uncle—"

"No, listen. This moping in self-pity has to stop. You're an adult. I let you have your space last semester to figure life out on your own. But it's the start of a new term. I won't let you squander your potential." He moved toward me, flame slanting on the muffin. "Here's the plan."

"Uncle Ben—"

"You'll attend every lecture and tutorial, and you'll return to the *Scribe*."

My throat tightened in dread and yearning.

Mostly dread.

"You'll write an article every week," he continued, "and by God you'll burn those sweatpants. Got it?"

"Uncle Ben—"

"Don't think of me as family. I am your leader, and it's time to follow my orders, kid."

I laughed incredulously. "Or what?"

"Or I'll make you pay rent."

That shut me up. That, and I was secretly thankful for the kick in the ass. "Won't miss a single class. I'll even take up another side project. But please don't make me work at the *Scribe*."

"Why not?"

Because Jack used to be there. Because Liam still was.

Hunter now, too.

Uncle Ben sighed. "Look, I know you think you messed up, Marc."

"I did mess up."

He nodded. "Accept it. Apologize. Don't let it define you."

My voice cracked. "Please, Uncle Ben—"

"I expect you at Wednesday's meeting. Until otherwise, I'm not Uncle Ben, I'm Chief Benedict. Your boss at the *Scribe*." He passed me the muffin and the melting candle. "Happy birthday, kid."

He left, and my shoulders slumped as I looked at the screen through the blur of the flickering flame. DaMage had sent me a picture of a cake with a twenty-two candle.

DaMage: Don't forget to make a wish.

I wish I could change the past.

But that was impossible. The most I could do was confront it.

I studied the bus-stop timetable taped to my bookshelf. If I left now, I could still make it.

To visit him in jail, or not to visit?

DaMage: You gonna slay demons?

I grabbed my jacket.

I was gonna slay demons.

I STARED AT MY DEMON.

He stared right back across a gray slate table, the white sleeves under his red inmate uniform bunched around thick forearms.

"You used to be the Jill to my Jack. Jack and Jill, we climbed every hill." Jack, ex-best friend, laughed drolly, while I cringed at my butchered surname and former nickname. "What happened to you, man?"

That should have been my line. Not his.

My grin ached. I gripped the plastic chair with sweaty palms. "I took up roleplaying and Cheetos."

"In Chief Benedict's basement?"

I scanned the dozen inmates greeting their visitors, the guards on duty, and lingered on Jack. "One of many ways to spell pathetic."

Another way? Having crushed on this abusive twenty-two-year-old now jailed for beating up gay guys—for threatening to kill last year's campus vigilante, the Raven.

Shame tightened its grip around my gut.

Jack stroked his new half-inch beard and cocked his head, gaze narrowed. "Why'd you come here, Jill?"

"Marc," I croaked, and hurriedly cleared my throat. "I go by Marc now."

"I only know Jill. Sassy smartass sidekick. One long-gone dad, a dead mother, and overall disappointment."

My feet jerked against the floor and the chair squealed. Guards turned in our direction. I smiled over gritted teeth, heat prickling my eyes. "Prison's changed you."

"No, it's freed me. No more tempering my thoughts. No more faking who I am." Jack leaned forward, bracing the table. "I'd tell you to try it, but I worry you'll try to jump my bones."

I winced. What did I ever see in him other than a Roman-like chiseled body, lazy confidence, and vast vocabulary?

Jack's bicep flexed and I flinched. Jack noted my flinch with the wry twist of his lips. "You were once a dad's worst nightmare. Trouble his daughter loved to indulge in. You wrote your number on their bras in permanent marker. Why'd you have to turn gay?"

I averted my eyes, gritting out a smile. I had always been gay. "I never did those things."

"You told me—"

"I told you a lot of things."

Jack's voice bowled toward me, punchy with disgust. "Why'd you want to visit?"

"You approved me."

"Sweatpants and an orange-stained T-shirt. Didn't exactly dress up for the occasion." His shrewd eyes narrowed. "You thought of skipping."

"I changed my mind at the last minute."

"Why?"

I arched a *You're-fucking-with-me* brow. "Why did I think of skipping a visit to the guy who beat me up for whispering how much I loved him in his ear?"

My stomach took a dive toward my feet.

"Why did you change your mind?"

Because it was my birthday wish.

My wish. To stand up for my sadly neglected principles. To say the words that drummed an insistent beat in my veins. To prove I still had *some* moral fiber.

I crossed my trembling arms. Sweat pearled under my bangs. My dry mouth tasted tinny.

Jack waited, eyes dark and lifeless.

Just like they'd been the moment after I'd whispered in his ear, before the first punch. Just like they'd been when I begged him to stop kicking me.

Fear froze my tongue.

I needed to slip on a mask of indifference. A grin would do it. It always did. "I came here because . . . because . . ."

"Because, because, because . . . Come on, get the hell on with it."

My grin hardened. "You attacked gay men. What you did was wrong."

Jack rolled his eyes. "Come on. We both did shit."

"I never hurt anyone."

"Maybe not physically. But you hurt people, Marc. You bullied Liam, you rubbed it into his face he has no friends; you snickered at his Aspergery ways; you hurt his feelings every day, and he wasn't the only disabled dude you gave shit to. You even flipped off the freak in the wheelchair."

Shame washed through me, pooled in my ears, hot and painful. "Hunter."

"Whatever, man." Jack caught my eye, held it hard. "You. Are. Just. Like. Me."

"No." It came out a wheeze smelling of dread.

Jack's nostril's flared. "You're right. You aren't just like me. You are *less*. I did everything because I love my brother. You did everything to impress *me*, a crush."

Heat rushed to my cheeks and I unlocked my jaw.

"Don't bother denying it, man. Anything else before your time's up? Want to confess your feelings again?"

My stomach revolted, flooding me with energy to drown the fear that his words conjured.

"Nah, dude. I am long over you." I pushed my chair back and scrounged up a wink. "I'll send you some birthday cake."

"You're full of bullshit."

My voice cracked. "No other way to survive life."

AT HOME, throat and eyes stinging, I threw myself at my desk. My screen was unlocked, my game still open. Cowering from life behind knighted armor and losing myself in fantasy worlds was the best thing I had going for me.

DaMage: One more thing.

DaMage: It doesn't seem right to know who you are while you don't know who I am.

DaMage: I gotta confess, I'm not sure you'll love the revelation.

My stomach twisted into fiery knots and I rubbed the screen like it might erase the truth.

DaMage: Hey, Marc Jillson. It's me. Travis Hunter.

CHAPTER TWO

I soaked in the impressive neo-Gothic facade of the Jefferson humanities building that housed the *Scribe* offices. Gray stone, arched windows, and steep-sloping roofs rose against a sunny sky. Gusty warm wind prompted me inside.

A deep laugh rang through the green-and-white tiled corridor. My step faltered as a funky electric thrill shot through my nauseated stomach.

A dozen yards away, waiting for the elevator, stood the two guys I most wanted to avoid. Liam Davis—tight-shouldered, Clark Kent lookalike—

And Hunter.

His wheelchair positioned him away from direct view but my mind conjured his face. Defined, strong jaw, straight hard nose, and a dimple on his right cheek. A dimple I'd only ever seen in profile.

Hunter. DaMage. One and the same.

Goosebumps shattered over me from scalp to feet.

I couldn't face him. Couldn't share the same elevator.

My shoe squealed as I pivoted back toward the entrance.

A swarm of literature students pouring out of a lecture hall blocked my path. Hunter, hand on his wheel, was about to turn—

I lurched behind a large potted palm, praying the ridiculously long leaves curtained me.

"Go ahead, Liam. I'll catch up."

Hunter's deep, calm voice carried down the rib-vaulted corridor.

Through the leaf gaps, I watched the elevator doors close on an inquisitive Liam, pen in hand, glasses pushed to the bridge of his nose.

Hunter waited a beat before spinning around and rolling down the corridor, gaze fixed on . . . my palm tree.

I'd been made.

I studied the leaves intently and begged the gods.

Roll past, roll past, roll . . .

"Jill."

Hunter cornered me. Dark, product-coiffed hair; tight fore-arms inked with hummingbird tattoos; a truckload of confidence glittering in blue eyes.

"What are you doing?" he asked, biceps flexing as he folded his arms.

I pinched a leaf, desperately searching for words. "Examining this plant for anthrax."

"Anthrax, eh? Without gloves?"

I lifted another leaf. "It's a fungal disease. Nasty. This palm is covered in it."

"Do you maybe mean anthracnose?"

That sounded better, yes. "That's the one."

"I see. Into plants, are you? Or are you working on campus as a caretaker now?"

Another leaf inspected. "Civic duty. I was taking initiative. I'll be reporting this anthracnose to the campus . . . people."

Hunter's mouth worked hard suppressing a laugh, and for the

first time I saw his dimple face-on. It punctuated his face with charisma, complementing eyes that danced with humor.

He leaned forward on his chair, voice creamy, smooth. "Show me your holes?"

My fingers slipped from the leaf so fast I cut myself. I swore and sucked on them, fighting the blazing heat in my cheeks. "My holes aren't for your eyes. Jesus, you're forward."

Hunter's brows shot up and he gestured to the potted palm. "The holes you found? The lesions? Anthracnose?"

Oh. "Right. Holes." I turned over a leaf. "Would you look at that. They disappeared. A miracle."

Hunter nodded thoughtfully. "Almost as miraculous as an indoor plant being infected with anthracnose in the first place." He eyed my tight jeans and even tighter T-shirt before rolling back a foot. "You're hiding from me."

I winced. It was true. "Or procrastinating seeing the chief?"

"You haven't played Demon-Slayage since Saturday."

"My computer broke?"

"You shrank in your Econ 302 seat when I came in yesterday."

"Unusually cold draught?"

He pinned me with a look that said he knew I was full of bull-shit. "We'd better move this upstairs. Meeting's about to start."

"You go ahead." I moved toward the next potted palm. "I'll just—"

His stern look had me sighing and reluctantly trailing him to the elevator. He paused at the opening doors. "After you, Jill."

"You called me Marc online."

"I guess I couldn't quite believe the guy I've been chatting with all summer is you."

"Yeah. Can you . . ."

Hunter side-eyed me. "Can I what?"

Keep calling me Marc? "Never mind."

WE ARRIVED at the conference room just in time. After Uncle Ben—ugh, Chief Benedict—told the crew in short words that I'd be back as reporter, he started the meeting. Nobody said anything or tried to catch my eye, and I returned the favor. Assignments allocated, the chief left. And so did the respectful quiet.

Hannah, writing for the Scribe's party page, tightened her long ponytail, accidentally elbowing my chin as we piled out of the conference room. "Sorry—oh, J-Jill." She stammered. Awkwardness stretched the foot between us, and I shrugged it off, determined to dump my belongings and hightail out of there.

Hannah courageously rolled her shoulders back. "So. Um. Where were you last semester?" A few other *Scribe* students listened in, and my heart steadily pumped aged guilt.

"You know, around."

She smiled and nodded. "Oh, yeah? Doing what?"

I smoothed on a grin and folded my arms, hoping my shoulders weren't bunched. "I was aiding some friends in an entrepreneurial fashion."

"Entrepreneurial?"

I should have guessed a journalist as good as Hannah would ask follow-up questions. "Concocting healing . . . beverages."

"That sounds . . ." She frowned. "Different. I thought I saw you a few weeks ago, under the Bridge of Sighs?"

The bridge that connected the courthouse to the prison. Yeah, I'd spent countless hours pacing the area, working up the courage to apply for a guest visit.

Everyone's inquisitive eyes rested on me. They were probably wondering if I was visiting Jack. If I was his henchman on the outside. If I was the same dick I was last year.

They seemed warily afraid of the answer. So was I. "Bridge of Sighs?" I murmured. "Might have been me. Had a few trips downtown with a hypnotist to help unlock the misplaced whereabouts of the final ingredient for those . . . beverages."

"Hypnotist?"

"Yeah. Quite the mission. But he helped me recall where I'd dried and stashed the mushrooms."

Hunter snorted and coughed into his elbow, and thankfully Hannah's phone rang.

I headed for my old desk and stopped—it was littered with rally posters and occupied by a large woman wearing a tight *There's No Planet B* T-shirt.

Hunter rolled beside me and slapped the back of my thigh. It tingled long after his hand disappeared. "Your new desk is by the shelves, next to mine."

"Yours?" My mouth dried and my nape immediately warmed. "Oh. I'll find somewhere else—"

"The only other free space is adjacent to Liam."

Red hot shame leaped to my cheeks. I didn't know what to say to Liam. Couldn't stand reliving every hurtful word I'd delivered, day in, day out. Even if I deserved it.

I looked from Hunter to Liam bowed over his desk, and back again.

I scoured the *Scribe* office for a third option. Every desk was crammed with books and laptops. Of course.

I sighed, mumbling to Hunter. "Lead the way."

Hunter studied me quietly as I arranged my desk, unpacking my dictionary and thesaurus and a folder of my favorite *Scribe* pieces.

Across the shiny table surface, Hunter's half of the desk was set up with camera equipment and chargers, printed photos, and a laptop port. For a moment, I wondered if he'd ever played Demon-Slayage here while I played in the basement in my sweatpants . . . or less than my sweatpants.

Fall breezes funneled through a cracked window across the room, reaching my flushed cheeks. I didn't dare peek at Hunter, but his clean, soapy scent carried toward me.

"Interesting summer you had," Hunter murmured. "Sounded

awfully like our Demon-Slayage mission to concoct a healing potion for Thief Gabriel."

I fished around my empty bag. "That obvious, huh?"

"What's up with the lies?"

Oh, come on. It wasn't obvious?

Hunter folded his arms and waited for my explanation.

I lowered my voice. "I know she asked, but no one really wants to hear how my life has been. I never earned their concern."

Hunter stilled, blue gaze softening. He leaned back in his wheelchair. "Okay. Ever thought about earning it?"

Every day. Every hour of every day. "After a year acting like a douche? You think—"

Liam approached Hunter, pushing up his glasses, and my skin burned. I frantically eyed escape. "—the vending machine sells gum? Cool. I'm gonna grab some."

I rushed out of the office.

The frosted glass sliding doors shut behind me and I collapsed for a breather against the wall opposite the elevators.

I ground my palm over my forehead and stopped. Emerging from the elevator was Tyler Bentley, one of the hottest IT nerds around. His golden hair was a ruffled mess and his jaw shimmered with stubble. His thriftshop-meets-catwalk style and bright eyes haunted me.

He'd been in most of my econ classes the last three years, and slinked around some of the best campus parties. But we'd rarely spoken. He tried once, after he caught me watching him on Halloween. He walked over nervously, dressed as Woody from Toy Story, and gave me ideas for the party page. That's when I'd learned he was deaf. His hands accompanied most of his sentences. I would have encouraged the chat if I hadn't been stupidly head-over-heels for Jack.

Christ. I shouldn't have brushed Tyler off. It'd taken guts for him to approach, and I'd gone right back to laughing with Jack.

I froze as his eyes caught on me and his lip hitched into a half-smile.

I managed a pathetic wave—about a second after he'd entered the *Scribe* offices.

"You are so smooth," I chastised myself, just as Hunter wheeled out into the hall and gave me a double take.

"Smooth?" He glanced over to where Tyler had disappeared. "Ahh." He grinned, eyes dancing. "Geek Force does it for you, huh?"

Hunter soaked in my defeated posture against the wall, and I wanted to melt into the lobby. Or scram out of there.

Liam stumbled from the office beside Hunter. "That Tyler is exceptionally odd."

The urge to defend the guy overcame me. "That's coming from you?"

Liam jerked his chin high, outwardly brushing off the insult. Regret knotted my stomach.

I opened my mouth to apologize but the words stuck in my throat.

Hunter, astute, beckoned Liam into the open elevator, suggesting they grab coffee at the Crazy Mocha. He swiveled around and rolled in backward. His gaze met mine, and he shook his head sadly.

CHAPTER THREE

I didn't know what the hell I did all week. The days slogged on, lectures too, and I spent more time than usual curled up in bed. Like I was now.

Bright light shafted through the basement windows across my face. I flung my arm over my eyes and groaned. I must've slept most of the day.

Uncle Ben was gonna charge my ass for missing two econ lectures. Worse than dipping into overdraft though? The disappointment that would cloud his face.

He was the only person still rooting for me, and letting him down . . .

My shitty character would be set in stone forever.

Here lies Marc Jillson

Unwaveringly consistent

Always the asshole

I fumbled for my phone under my tear-splotched pillow. Three-thirty in the afternoon!

Shit.

I showered in four minutes and dressed in two. Maybe if I

could borrow someone's notes, I could recover from my absences? Chief would never have to know.

Except, dammit!

My article was due this evening.

My campus news article. The article I'd meant to figure out today.

I slung my laptop-heavy bag over my shoulder and raced to campus.

I made it to the econ department five minutes before my final class. Puffing outside the hall's atrium doors, I jabbed my phone and made a call.

"Hey, Chief."

Uncle Ben hummed suspiciously. "Marc."

I winced, stealing into the fluorescent, chatty atrium. "Can I have an extension on my article? A couple of hours?"

A dry laugh. "When have I ever given you preferential treatment?"

"Now would be nice?"

Uncle Ben paused. "Your voice seems fine and as of last night, no injuries I know about."

I raced down the middle aisle toward vacant seats in the front, stalling when I realized I plunked down next to geek-boy-hottie Tyler. I jerked my gaze away, groaning internally. Hunter was typing away on his laptop.

I sank into my seat as far as I could go, whispering, "One hour extra? Please?"

"I expect your piece at six. On time, like everyone else's."

"It's four."

"Better get cracking then."

So much for paying attention to the professor. All my notebook scribbles were random ideas I could pull out of my ass for *Scribe*.

Tyler spent the lecture diligently staring at his phone screen where his stenographer—a raven-haired woman in her thirties—

sent him real-time captions to the lecture. I'd vaguely known he had help writing notes for his classes, but I had never witnessed the stenographer's instant and accurate translation.

When classes ended, his stenographer packed her things and signed to him. He signed back and watched her leave.

He turned his dark eyes on me, grinning. "Find that fascinating, Marc?"

The cadence of his voice was deep and slightly off, but intelligence and humor marked his expression.

I lifted my hands and signed.

He laughed. "You said you have shit for brains."

I nodded and spoke clearly so he could read my lips. "Yes. It's the only sentence I know. Also, it's true."

He laughed. "You didn't take notes—and you didn't show to our other two lectures."

I signed my one sentence again. He laughed.

Sudden inspiration had me bolting to my feet. Maybe I could interview Tyler? Learn about how he navigates his classes as a person hard of hearing. "Can I make a copy of your notes and ask some questions in exchange for coffee?"

Across the room, Hunter laughed and the sound drummed a hiccupy beat in my chest. I glanced over, admiring that deep dimple and those glittering eyes. The guy he conversed with wore the tightest pair of red jeans I'd ever seen and stared at Hunter with a flirtatious smirk, body language all but begging for a hookup.

Hunter winked and both their cell phones came out. Something glugged around in my stomach and I shoved the feeling as deep as I could, rushing Tyler out of the atrium at his eagerness for coffee.

We lined up at the freestanding coffee cart by large windows overlooking hundreds of students crisscrossing the campus. The scent of coffee percolated the corner.

"So, tell me about yourself, Tyler."

Tyler blushed. "Yeah, okay."

The customers in front of us left and we stepped up. I met Tyler's eye and gestured to the cart and the bored, rainbow-haired student running it. "Go nuts, it's on me. Grab a drink for each hand."

"One black coffee will do."

Rainbow Hair pumped Tyler a paper cup of coffee and handed it over.

I eyed the menu. "What do I want? What do I want?"

"There are literally two options," Tyler said, frowning.

I grinned at him. "Which makes it a fifty percent chance I choose the wrong thing."

A deep, familiar chuckle sounded from behind me and I froze.

Hunter rolled to my other side, eyes curiously scrolling down Tyler. "He'll have the coffee."

"Will he?" Tyler asked.

Hunter leaned forward as if to pass on a secret. "He's a fan. Last year his *Scribe* desk was littered with coffee cups."

Heat walloped to my cheeks. "What are you talking about?"

Hunter's gaze settled on me, and my stomach twisted with nerves. Something about Hunter made it seem like he saw right through me. Like he saw every guilty corner and yet refused to pass judgment. "You also have a definitive coffee scent about you."

A half-baked laugh blubbered out of me and I stuffed my hands into my pockets. "Ah, you mean a bright, caffeinated aura?"

"Or an over-caffeinated nervous twitch." Hunter glanced toward Tyler and back, eyes twinkling. "Sorry for interrupting your date."

I jerked my hands out of my pockets, shaking my head hard. "I'm not on a—this is not a date."

Tyler made a soft noise and dropped his eyes to the steaming coffee cup in his hand.

My palms pearled with sweat, and my throat felt sticky. He thought this was a date?

I mean, a date! I wanted that. And Tyler was exceptionally hot. Was it too late to take it back? "He was about to tell me all about himself."

Tyler took a step backward, coffee spilling over his hand. "I just remembered, I have a meeting with my tutor. Thanks for the coffee."

Well, fuck. That didn't go well. "Tyler—"

"Later."

I chastised myself.

Rainbow Hair cleared her throat. "Tea or coffee?"

Hunter cocked his head. I stared at him and that ridiculously deep dimple. Rainbow Hair asked again, and when Hunter leaned toward her to answer on my behalf, I blurted. "Tea."

Rainbow Hair gaped at me. "Black or fruity?" She lifted two boxes of tea from under the cart—one unopened box of Earl Grey, and one dusty box of Fruit Sensation.

"Does the black have caffeine in it?" I asked hopefully. Hunter smirked. "Never mind. Fruity is good. Fruity is so what I want."

I paid for my tea and long-gone Tyler's coffee, and Hunter ordered two coffees with a splash of milk in a paper carrier.

I fixed a protective cardboard sheath around my cup and surreptitiously eyed the benches along the windows for Hunter's Red Jeans wannabe hookup.

Hunter balanced the coffee carrier on his lap, rolling in my direction, the fastest way out of there.

"Where's your date?" I asked.

"At my place—later. I'm heading to *Scribe*. Like you should be."

Yeah, if I had anything to submit.

Hunter side-eyed me. "Were you about to pump Tyler for an article?"

"Jesus, that sounds crass. I was going to ask him some questions about how he navigated university. But mostly I was after his lecture notes."

"Yeeeeah. Jill? That's not any less crass."

My shoulders slumped when I heard it. Fuck. I scrubbed my jaw. "You got me." I blew on my tea, took a sip, and promptly spat it back into the cup. "God, that's disgusting."

I walked through the sliding doors and dumped the tea right into the nearest trash.

Hunter kept pace, rolling alongside. "You didn't brainstorm a campus story?"

I sighed. "I didn't do crap this week, okay? I spent most of it half-naked, ripping into a jumbo-sized bag of Cheetos, grieving the loss of Demon-Slayage." Hunter's chair stalled and I jerked around. "You okay?"

"That was quite a picture you painted." He blinked me in from head to toe and my skin fritzed with electricity. "You know you could come back to the game."

I laughed. "Right. Because DaMage and Fawkes will pick up right where they left off."

"It'll be an adjustment. I get it."

I grunted.

Hunter peered at me, quizzically. "Jumbo bag of Cheetos?"

"I have an addiction."

Hunter rolled smoothly past me. "Genetics were very kind to you. Come. I have an idea for your story. I'll even take a few pictures for you to fill out your article."

"Really?" I pointed to his coffee carrier. "But you're meeting someone." Liam?

Hunter handed me a coffee, laughing softly. "I refuse to believe you have shit for brains."

My breath hitched. He'd heard that with Tyler?

My hand curled around the warm cup and I followed after Hunter, sipping quietly.

———

"Your article is right around the corner."

"Shit. I don't think. I've ever. Been to this. Hill. On campus."

"Yes. It sounds like you should climb it more often. Maybe also check out the university gym."

"Fuck." I paused to puff, eying Hunter. It had to be bicep-aching work rolling his chair up this zigzag path. "Why haven't you broken a sweat?"

"Gym. Physio. Basketball. A diet rich in vegetables and light on cheesy chips."

I groaned and continued the uphill struggle. "There goes any future for us."

Hunter laughed.

At the top of the hill, Hunter veered down a narrow adjacent path fringed with wild roses. A posted wooden sign, half covered by tree branches, read Lover's Loop.

"Lover's Loop?" I followed him, gulping in sweetly-perfumed air. "What is this article supposed to look like, exactly?"

"Like this." Hunter pointed at an antique wooden gazebo. Octagonal, with a turret-shaped, shingle-layered roof. Pretty, in the wild garden setting. Pretty romantic.

Hunter rolled up a ramp into the gazebo. He swiveled his chair toward me and opened his arms wide. "Built in the eighteen-eighties." He gestured to the ramp. "Modified in the nineties." He grinned. "A well-kept secret hideout. Usually used by lovers."

So the bushes were probably littered with used condoms? I modified pretty romantic to pretty gross.

I cautiously joined him inside, breezes buffered by a white trellis decorated with mini padlocks.

Hunter uncapped his camera lens and snapped pictures. In the shadows of the gazebo, light from the screen hit his gently smiling face.

I leaned against a support beam. "If it's a well-kept secret, why would you want *Scribe* readers knowing about it?"

Hunter lifted his camera and took a shot of me. He drew the camera down, holding it against his chest, gaze meeting mine.

"They're planning to tear it down. Replace all this with modern benches and pansy beds. A small group is lobbying against the change. You could encourage students to help save it."

I withdrew my phone, opened my email, and jotted notes. "Why is it important to you?" I asked, glancing toward the trellis. "Is one of these forever-in-love padlocks yours?"

"My parents'."

I stopped typing. "Really?"

"Not a padlock. Their initials are scratched on the beam behind me." Hunter slid his camera into the bag slung over his chair, and rolled backwards—

The sickening *knack* of splitting wood cut through the air, and Hunter's chair dropped sharply to one side.

I lunged across the gazebo, dropping my phone, and desperately clutched the arm of the wheelchair before it plunged any deeper into the rotting wood.

My muscles strained to hold the heavy weight. "Bet those pansy beds are looking good about now."

Hunter barked a laugh between uncharacteristic curses. "Could you come behind me and pull toward your left?"

I rounded the chair and pulled. Heaved. Vowed to climb more hills and visit the gym.

The wheelchair finally dislodged and found purchase on the slat floors. At the edge of the concrete ramp, I let go of his chair, palmed my knees, and caught my ragged breath.

Hunter set his lips in a grim line. "I hope this doesn't change your mind about saving the gazebo."

"Jesus. It nearly eats you and you still want to save it?"

I felt his eyes shift from the wreck inside to me. The hairs on my nape prickled.

"It needs tender loving care," he said. "Strengthen the foundation and I'm certain its beauty will prevail." I attempted eye contact but he fixed his gaze on the gazebo floor. "What do you think?"

"I think," I said, stealing inside, veins skipping with shivers, "I lost my phone."

Cautiously, I lowered myself to the cool grainy slats and peered into the hole. Dark forms lurked in darker shadows. "Great. I can't see my phone without my phone."

"Here. Use mine."

Hunter shook his phone and bright light blasted out.

I crawled back for it, and Hunter set it in my upturned palm, curling my fingers around it. His fingers so much warmer than my own. I stared at my hand for a ridiculously long beat.

"Jill?"

I threw myself toward the hole. Perhaps aimed to dive into it.

I angled Hunter's light. Shadows—and spiders—leaped aside, revealing debris and my phone face down on an old rectangular tin.

I pulled both out and rolled onto my back. A sticky glob of dust dropped onto my face and I spluttered as I sat upright.

Hunter raised a brow. I held out his phone, careful to pinch it so our skin wouldn't brush.

"Yeah, I need you to put your number in there before you give it back to me."

My gaze—trained on the phone—jerked to his. "My number? What for?"

"I'm not sure yet." Hunter gripped his phone and unlocked the screen. "Put it in my address book."

With a weird hop in my stomach, I plugged in my details and handed back his phone. He thumbed the screen, frowned, and peered over it at me. "Okay."

I quickly returned to inspecting the tin box, wiping through a greasy layer of dust.

"What did you find?" he asked.

"A vintage tin box."

"What's inside it?"

"Does it matter? This is an Archie tin."

Hunter plucked the tin out of my grip with a smirk. "A scratched-up Archie tin." He shook it gently and something shifted inside. His eyes danced. "I'm definitely curious what's inside."

I pushed to my feet, and he handed the tin back to me, not immediately releasing his hold. "If you want to show me."

"I . . . Ah . . . Uh huh. We need a property service for some fact-checking. Time's ticking."

Hunter rolled back and fanned an arm out. "Lead the way, Marc."

──────────

CHAPTER FOUR

──────────

arc.

Hunter's soft utterance of my name followed me the rest of the evening. It felt promising. Like maybe I could start with a clean slate.

I stared at my computer. Did I dare go back on Demon-Slayage?

I groaned as I clicked into the game. I wanted to be on here. Badly.

Nervous butterflies hit my stomach. Hunter was already online.

DaMage: You're back!

Me: I'm not sure this is a good idea.

DaMage: In light of us knowing each other?

Me: It was more fun when you didn't know the real me.

DaMage: Are you worried I'm judging you?

Me: Aren't you?

I tapped my desk nervously, waiting for his reply.

DaMage: Maybe it's not a bad thing?

Me: Finding out what a shit I am in real life?

DaMage: Finding out there are other sides to you.

Me: Other sides. Right.

DaMage: We've been gaming together all summer. I've noted a couple redeeming qualities.

Me: Like my stunning ability to lead us into a demon trap, only to lose my sword and depend on you to magic our way out of it?

DaMage: For example.

I groaned and lounged back in my desk chair, staring at the chat screen.

DaMage: You're also disarmingly funny.

I wrote a bunch of responses that I immediately deleted. I gnawed on my lip, typed out another reply, and hit send before I could second-guess myself.

Me: How did your date with Red Jeans go?

Maybe I should have second-guessed myself.

DaMage: Red Jeans?

Me: Yeah, were they colored or was it blood from being so damn tight?

DaMage: I should have taken them off for a better look.

Me: Next time.

DaMage: Maybe. Not sure there'll be a next time.

Me: He didn't do it for you?

DaMage: Maybe for a few no-strings fucks. But . . . We'll see.

Me: . . .

DaMage: You asked.

Me: You answered.

DaMage: Kind of the way questions work. Got any others?

Yes. A lot, actually. None I knew how to ask.

Me: Let's just find the Amulet of Redemption and be quick about it.

DaMage: I have a question. What's in the Archie tin?

Me: I haven't opened it yet.

DaMage: You're killing me. OPEN IT.

Me: Help me with these venomous demons and I will. Hell, I'll personally deliver it and let you do the honors.

DaMage threw a cluster of seriously powerful potions at our enemies. He must have been saving up for a long time because every demon in a five-mile radius froze.

Me: The fuck?

DaMage: 156 Walnut Ave, ground floor, apartment 2A.

DaMage: Wait, you don't drive. What's your address?

I BURST upstairs into Uncle Ben's apartment. He was sitting at the dining table in the glow of his laptop. Checking out my *Scribe* submission, no doubt.

He peered over the screen. "They're pulling down the gazebo at Lover's Loop?"

He knew the place? "Yeah. In three weeks. Where's the vacuum cleaner?"

Uncle Ben lowered his screen, expression morphing quizzically. "The vacuum?"

"I want to clean." I checked the grandfather clock adjacent to him. "Immediately."

"Surely that means stuffing everything from the floor into your closet?"

Well, yes. But. "I need to do a thorough job. Vacuum the carpet. Run all-purpose cleaner over the bathroom . . ."

Uncle Ben scrubbed the surprise off his face. "The vacuum is in the hallway cupboard, along with sprays. You don't expect me to help, do you?"

"Stop acting like this is the first time I've cleaned."

"Voluntarily, it is."

"Well, it might become a thing. Get used to it."

"Sure. If the urge arises, my place can be used for practice."

"Funny."

"So, who is he?"

"Who?"

"Who you're cleaning for?"

"It's not enough to clean for myself?"

"At nine-thirty on a Thursday night?"

"You should have been a detective," I mumbled, hoofing to the hall for cleaning items. Uncle Ben's laughter followed me.

Back in my basement apartment, I collected my laundered but unfolded laundry and stuffed it into my closet, vacuumed the floor, and gunned all-purpose spray on every surface.

My phone buzzed in my pocket.

Hunter: Any stairs to negotiate?

Me: Nope. On a hill though, path descends to the back of the house. I'm in the basement.

I stashed the vacuum, sprays, and half-eaten Cheetos bag in the closet with the laundry before dashing my hands through soapy water.

The doorbell dinged, and I swept open the door to a startled Hunter.

The sensor light glowed over his spiked hair, snug-fitting shirt, dark jeans, and bright blue Nike's. He always carried himself with enviable composure, and now was no different. He sat tall, hands resting lightly on his wheels, bright eyes holding mine with a pleased twinkle.

"Hey," I said.

"Hi."

"Yep, heya."

Hunter cracked a grin. "Going to let me in?"

"Sure. Just saying hello. In all its variations, apparently." I held the door wide open.

He steered into the room, hauling in a deep breath. "Huh. Clean."

"Yeah, that's totally me," I said, shutting the door on a chilled breeze.

Hunter smirked as he rolled toward my desk, where my computer slept. Where I'd spent the summer chatting online with him, learning random facts. The last two books he'd read were from Jamie Oliver and Dan Brown. His favorite meals involved pasta, and he once contemplated the merits of becoming a Pastafarian at the Church of the Flying Spaghetti Monster.

I held out the Archie tin. "There you go. Enjoy. Maybe return the tin when you're done?"

Hunter breathed in the lavender grove scented air. "You want me to piss off already?"

No.

I stared at the tin he refused to take from me. "You want to stay?"

Hunter answered by rolling past me. He positioned his chair and gracefully slung himself onto the couch. "Bring it here, we'll look together." He patted the spot next to him.

I sat on the furthest end of the couch feigning fascination with the tin box, feeling the prickly heat of Hunter's gaze on me. "The tin won't open."

"I don't bite, Marc." He paused. "Usually."

"Ha! It's just, I have a . . . bad back. Yeah. And this corner doesn't sag."

Hunter's stern look told me to quit the bullshit and scoot, pronto.

I sighed and scooted.

Heat radiated into my side, and I tried opening the tin again. Mission impossible with stupid, shaky hands.

Hunter eased the tin out of my grip and had a go. "Tricky to get into, all right."

With a *pop* the lid came clean off its hinges, and the back of Hunter's hand bashed into my face.

My hands flew to my aching nose.

Hunter winced, twisting his torso toward me.

"You broke it," I grunted through the pain.

"Your nose?"

I dropped my hands. "The tin!"

Laughter broke through Hunter's sympathetic expression. "The tin I can fix." He cradled my cheek and my body froze, nerve endings suspended. His thumb tenderly brushed over the bridge of my nose. "Looks okay. Might bruise."

His gaze flickered to mine, and he slowly released me. He turned his attention to the contents of the tin, while I regrouped my soupy interior.

"Letters," Hunter murmured. "Dozens of letters."

He pulled them out onto his lap and studied them, many spoiled by leaked tin water. Or perhaps the author's tears.

Hunter sorted them by date, and I pinched the one at the top of the pile and read.

Sep 1972

Dear V,

You always loved to start a conversation with humor. So I'll joke, to set the tone right:

Jojo had puppies. I kept one and named her Triplets so that when people ask for favors I can say I'm busy caring for triplets.

I also like how it sounds. I'm a man who might have kids, even though you and I know that will never happen.

I mean that, V. It will never happen.

My family is respected—there will always be pressure to hide—but I will not commit myself to a loveless marriage. You are the one I love. The one I wish I could bring home to one of our fancy parties. This is V.A., the love of my life, my forever . . .

Oh, V. It pains me that you're the one I've hurt the most.

The one I denied in such ruthless fashion.

The one I turned away to fight a war I've been protected from.

I am so desperately sorry.

Yours always,

K

"Are they all from K?" I asked.

"Looks like it. All to this V guy."

"Can you be sure V is a guy?"

Hunter passed me another letter.

Oct. 1972

Dear V,

I wish I could send my last letter to you, but I know it could land you in trouble. I also don't deserve your forgiveness.

Yet I dream about you granting it to me daily. Hourly. Every damn minute.

Remember when we first met?

I'd rushed out of my dorm room without an umbrella and the clouds opened up on me. I used my backpack to shield my head and dashed under the gazebo. I swore colorfully when I saw my soaked notebook.

I heard your laugh first. Deep, melodic, gentle. I was startled to find I wasn't alone. You were sitting in the shadows, on the flat bench beside the trellis. Dark hair dripping water over the most handsome face I'd ever seen. I couldn't stop staring, and your laugh turned nervous. You asked whose notes I'd lost and I told you Professor Fiend's.

The most miraculous smile lit your face as you dug out notes from the same class.

I think I fell in love with you in those first minutes. And by God, I'd come back to this gazebo at the same time every morning to see if we met again. And we did. Every morning, without fail, you were there. Our conversations were always packed with humor, light, yet hope glittered at the edges. After that first month, when I finally gathered the courage to ask you to my baseball game—

God, I'll never forget. You and me in the gazebo. Your rogue smile, the determined way you stepped close to me, your hands soft on my jaw, your warm lips closing over mine. Your murmur: Yes, and after can we go someplace private?

"It's still not a hundred percent conclusive." Although I had imagined two men while I read it.

"I've got a pretty decent gaydar."

I lifted a brow. "That works on letters?"

He gave a lazy shrug. "I sense these things."

"Is that how you figured out I'm gay?" Because I certainly hadn't told him.

Hunter glared at me, lip curling. "I caught you checking me out last year."

"Pfft. That's . . . No way." I sliced my gaze away, but a shivery zap shot through me, and I became ultra-aware of how close Hunter was. His soft soapy scent with a hint of olive, the careful way his large hands sorted through yellowed letters, his curious hums.

He passed me another letter.

Dec. 1972

Dearest V,

I've written letters to you every week. Failed to send them every week also.

I've run out of jokes, dear V.

I don't know if I could laugh again if I tried.

I can't sleep.

When I do, we are gathered up with all the boys at the bar, crouched before the TV watching the live broadcast of the lottery. My stomach is in knots. My whole body strung out on fear. I know your number better than my own. When they called it out . . . On my grave, V, I swear I begged the universe to trade places with you. My heart shattered that day. I never wanted to stop making love to you that night, and all the ones we had left.

I wish you hadn't graduated so you could defer.

When you came over to kiss me goodbye that last time . . . I wish we hadn't been caught.

I will never forgive myself for denying you in front of my mother. You should never forgive me for shoving you out in the cold.

I didn't live up to my promise to be true to myself, no matter the obstacle.

I was scared.

Scared and stupid and oh so sorry.

"Fine. The clues add up." I reread the letter with a sympathetic twist in my gut. I couldn't imagine how frightening it must have been to be drafted. Jesus, they were probably our age. Barely beginning to navigate adulthood. "Seems like K fucked up his goodbye. Wonder if he was forgiven?"

Hunter finished perusing another letter. "There's no answer in here. Just these dozen letters."

"Think that means V died?" I speedread the letters, hoping for a happy ending where V forgave K for being an asshole and they lived happily ever after.

I sighed and dropped them into the broken tin on Hunter's lap. I dropped my head back against the couch. "Well that was fun."

Hunter mirrored me, smiling sadly. "Love is fleeting. At least they had it for a moment."

And if I didn't think the night could get more depressing . . .

"With that attitude, why do you even care to save Lover's

Loop gazebo? Did your parents separate? Are you clinging to some hope they'll be reunited?"

"My parents are the only exception I know. They met at the gazebo." He gave a self-deprecating laugh. "Maybe saving it will ensure their love forever? Maybe it'll help me find my own? I don't know."

"You don't need help finding love. Not the way you sweet-talked Red Jeans." Not with his massive amount of confidence.

"I have a lot of first, second, and third dates. Not many fourth."

I palmed my nape. "I've never been on a proper date with a guy. Well, supposedly there was Tyler earlier, but it escaped my notice. Doubt he'll go for a second."

"Have you ever been intimate with a guy before?"

"Yeah." I flushed. "Grindr."

"I hope your partners were good to you."

I shrugged. "It's always to the point. You know, get dicked and get home."

Hunter frowned.

Thankfully, a sharp knock sounded on the door that led upstairs. I bolted to my feet and stuffed my hands in my pockets. "Yeah?"

Uncle Ben entered, took one look at my boiling face and Hunter on the couch. His face blasted with a smile. "Sorry for the interruption. I broke a glass. Can I use the vacuum?"

"Sure." I eyed the closet and a frowning Hunter, who had a direct view of it. Ah, hell. "Maybe glass is better swept up? Little shards might ruin the vacuum interior . . . bits."

Uncle Ben's get-to-it-quick look had me reluctantly opening the closet.

Out tumbled the Cheetos bag, followed by the sprays. In my effort to stabilize the vacuum, I nudged the laundered heap and everything spewed out in a mound of messy.

I burned under Hunter's gaze.

Uncle Ben winced with sympathy and hurried off with his vacuum. I debated stuffing my clothes back into the closet, or giving up and leaving them in their natural habitat.

I gathered an armful and tossed it back into the closet. "I'm a disgusting mess, okay?"

Hunter blinked at me.

"Fuck. Say something."

Hunter snapped out of his glazed stare. "You live under Chief Benedict?"

Huh? Oh. "He's my uncle. Ben."

Hunter stared in disbelief. "You kept that close to the sleeve."

I shrugged. "Didn't want people at *Scribe* thinking I'm a privileged asshole. Probably because I am one. Guess you'll read my articles differently now?"

Hunter shook out of the last of his shock. "That's assuming I've read them at all."

I ran a hand through my hair. "Oh. Ha. Don't bother."

"I have read them. Binge-read them the day after I discovered who I'd been hanging out with online all summer."

"You did?"

"Yes." A beeping sounded and Hunter checked his phone. He swiveled his chair close. "I've gotta hit the road."

"Oh." I moved out the way and he moved into his chair. "Sure thing."

He glanced toward my closet and back at me, grinning. "Thanks for giving me a glimpse inside . . . the tin."

Fuck. Hunter was smart. Hunter was funny and smart, and I didn't want the night to end. But now we knew what was in . . . the tin, I guess that was it. We'd go back to the way things were. Back to sort of knowing each other. To nodding in passing.

I'd go back to watching Hunter hang out with Liam.

Hunter wheeled toward the back door.

"I flipped you off once," I blurted, and Hunter paused, back facing me. "That's a lie. I flipped you off a few times, back when Jack and I . . ."

"Yeah."

"It was stupid. You got under my skin."

"I know."

"You're right about me checking you out. I did."

Hunter hummed.

"I'm sorry," I said.

"For checking me out? Or for flipping me off?"

"Both?"

"You know, it's not me you need to apologize to, Marc."

That was Liam.

I scuffed a socked foot over the hardwood floor.

Hunter shifted his grip on his wheels, and I sidled past him, reluctantly opening the door. "Have a good night."

He rolled out into the cool night, and turned his chair. "I almost forgot." He rummaged into the bag slung over his chair, pulled out a sheaf of stapled paper, and handed it to me.

"What's this?"

"You missed a couple of classes today."

I clasped the printed copy of Hunter's notes, my chest hitching. "Thank you."

He nodded and wheeled down the brick path.

I shut the door and slumped against it, rubbing the edge of Hunter's notes against my cheek, where he'd touched me. "Why do I suddenly feel lonely?" I whispered.

A heavy *bang-bang* met the door and I lurched back and yanked it open, heart skipping.

Hunter stared at me, frustrated. "Can I have the contents of the tin?"

"You're not done with it?"

"Aren't you curious to find answers? An ending to the story?"

The intensity of Hunter's stare made me shiver deep in my bones.

I retreated into the room, and returned clutching the tin. "What if it's disappointing?"

He paused. "I'll take the risk."

"It'll be hard work, finding everything out."

"I've never been afraid of hard work."

I swallowed and stared at the tin. "Maybe I can help you? We could figure out this mystery relationship together?"

Hunter's smile dazzled, and the edges of the tin cut into my hand I held it so hard.

"Who knows," I said, handing the tin to Hunter. "Maybe we could work the angle that Lover's Loop is a historical landmark and should be protected by the university . . ."

"I do also want to save the gazebo." Hunter didn't take the tin. "Since we'll be working together, you should keep it."

I clasped it against my chest. "Okay. Good."

"Good."

"Excellent."

"Fantastic."

I laughed. "Are you leaving now?"

"Sure." Hunter winked. "Just saying how happy this makes me. In all its variations, apparently."

CHAPTER FIVE

Ten minutes before our only shared Friday lecture, I was such a pathetic ass I kept straightening every time the atrium doors opened and a new horde of students piled in. The clock ticked four, and that made it nine hours my stomach had been in knots.

When Hunter rolled in, he was immediately accosted by Red Jeans, who was wearing blue jeans.

Hunter's gaze landed on me, and he nodded. A friendly nod? Or casual acquaintance nod?

Red Jeans stole his attention until Professor Velazquez launched into her lecture. Hunter dove into typing notes.

My phone buzzed in my pocket, an unfamiliar vibration after so many months of silence.

I surreptitiously fished it out.

Unknown: I have another confession.

I saved the contact and answered. Hunter kept his head bowed toward his screen.

Hunter: Last night. I wasn't surprised at the hidden mess. I'd guessed you cleaned up.

Me: You guessed?

Hunter: There was an acidic lavender scent clinging to you. Usually you smell earthy.

Earthy? Was that a euphemism for dirty? I might tend towards the slobby, but I showered every day. Sometimes more than once. I glared at the screen.

Me: Well you smelled like soap and a stupid amount of fresh air.

Across the atrium, Hunter peeked at me over his laptop and I sank into my seat.

Hunter: Earthy wasn't an insult, Marc. I like it.

Hunter: I also really like that you cleaned. For me.

Me: That's what you do when you have guests over. I'm not a complete Neanderthal.

Me: I'm also not the biggest fan of your confessions.

Even across the room, Hunter's smirk sparked an electric frisson in my chest.

Hunter: After class I'm grabbing coffee with Liam, then I have a Skype date with my sister (she's on an exchange in Germany).

Me: . . .

Hunter: Don't be disappointed when we don't chat.

Me: Disappointed?

I scoffed.

Me: Piss off.

But as soon as the lecture finished and Hunter rolled out, a heavy wave tumbled over me.

I headed to *Scribe* where I'd brought the tin box, and sat at my desk, pondering how to save the gazebo. Maybe I could interview the protesters? Or lure stories from past lovers . . .

Hannah sidled up to my desk with a tentative smile, a Goliath cautiously watching from behind her. Times like these, I wished I could wave my gay badge.

"Hannah?"

"You've been here for hours, staring at Hunter's desk."

I shifted uncomfortably. "Yeah, so?"

She rocked back, and I chastised myself for the attitude.

"It's Friday night. You used to love parties."

I used to love Jack. Things change.

"Rumor has it there's a secret party in the storage room behind the library. Roger and I are checking it out. Want to come?"

"How do students get in after hours?"

"Apparently some girl Daisy has a key card. Maybe a staff kid scored it? Not sure how long it will go before campus security close it down, but I'm chasing after an article."

"Sounds like it'll be a good one."

She flushed. "Thanks. That means a lot, coming from you."

It did?

"God, I'd love it if you checked out one of my party pieces and gave me advice."

My throat tightened weirdly, and I nodded. "Sure. Uh, but you're a good writer, Hannah. I'm sure I won't have much to say."

Hannah left blushing, and I returned to staring at the tin—and Hunter's desk.

And the tin again.

I pulled out the letters and studied them all a third time.

I wedged my phone from my pocket.

I had an idea.

Hunter waited under lamppost light, wearing an open jacket with the figure of DaMage on his T-shirt. His face was turned toward drunken student laughter, in profile to me.

Strong jaw and smoothly shaved cheeks, like a classically handsome *geek* statue. I swaggered toward him, and his gaze hit me with a shiver. A star eying a slutty fan in a knight-print shirt—and the tightest pair of jeans I owned.

Hunter eyed me up and down with a rogue smile. "Why'd you ask me here?"

"Because of your confession."

"About cleaning up for me?" He cocked his head and studied my face when I paused before him.

I averted my gaze and swallowed thickly. "Your *other* confession. Last week. About being a Geek Force God."

"God? You are so good for my ego." I caught him smirk. "What about it?"

I hitched a thumb towards the union link. "Follow me."

Hunter kept pace beside me as we smuggled ourselves into the secret party. Shelves of outdated books and old computers mazed around us, and about fifty guys and girls paraded around aisles with red cups.

I didn't spot Hannah.

Students nicked their heads at us in casual hello. "Dude."

"Dude."

A guy with oily auburn hair and a shirt open to an equally oily chest raised his cup to us. "Hey, man on wheels. So, like, how do you piss?" His chuckle morphed into a stage whisper. "Can you still get it up? Do you feel anything down there?"

Hunter calmly met his eye with a charming grin. "Hey, guy-I've-never-met-before. Get to know me first and I'll gladly tell you anything you want to know."

"Oh shit," some girl said, laughing. "Steve just got burned."

I gritted my teeth, angry at shithead Steve for rudely asking the question. Angrier that I'd wondered the same thing and hoped Hunter might answer. "Should we leave?"

Hunter pinned me with an appraising look before wheeling toward the keg. "Shit like this happens from time to time. I'm not cowering away. Why'd you want me here?"

I scoured the crowd. "This girl Daisy has a key card into the union link. That card also opens up the library. I thought we can sneak in and browse the 1972 yearbook. Narrow down all male students whose names start with V and later cross reference them with those that were drafted."

"You know the library opens on Saturday, right?"

"Yeah."

"So why are we here tonight?"

I don't want to hang out another Friday night alone. The thought came like a punch, unbidden yet powerful. I forced a lazy smirk over my discomfort. "I'm impatient. Want to call it quits?"

Hunter poured a red plastic cup of beer and handed it to me. "So you lured me here for a sleuthing mission?"

"You brought your computer, right? You can do the cross-referencing."

"Is that right?"

"Yep."

"Marc?"

"Yep?"

"You're allowed to look at me."

My face heated, and I hid in a slow sip of cool beer. "I've looked at you." Quick glimpses. "We need to focus on finding Daisy. I'll keep my eyes on the prize."

"I don't promise to do the same."

What? I whisked toward him, gaze snagging with Hunter's.

He smiled. "Better. I rather like those pretty hazel eyes on me."

"They're brown. Not hazel. Definitely not pretty."

"You'll need to stare at me a while to verify that."

My skin tightened. Everywhere.

I gripped my cup so hard beer splashed over the rim and over my hand. "Fuck."

Hunter's gaze landed behind me. "I think I spotted Miss Daisy."

That was our girl all right. The daisies in her hair were on the nose, but totally worked in our favor. The key card we needed peeked out of her ass pocket.

"Follow my lead, Hunter." I fiddled with my phone as I veered toward her.

She and her friend caught my approach and Daisy's mouth dropped open. Her friend whispered in her ear, and Daisy blushed, dark eyes blinking me in.

"Sorry to interrupt," I said.

Her friend giggled. "You're not interrupting."

Daisy's stern look had her friend scooting down the aisle. Daisy smiled. "You're not interrupting."

I gave her my smoothest smile. Hunter, beside me, watched with rapt interest.

I casually tapped the padded arm of his chair, gesturing for Hunter to go around Daisy and steal the key card.

Hunter snatched my fingers in what I guessed was defiance.

Goodbye plan A.

Daisy's gaze flashed from me to Hunter, and I cleared my

throat. "I'm Marc, that's Hunter."

After a moment of confusion, her face bloomed fuchsia. "Oh. Two of you. Marc, my ex's name. Uh, I mean, nice. And Hunter, that's unusual."

"My parents had little imagination." I inclined my head toward Hunter. "His parents caught him tearing after his sister snapping his teeth as a baby."

Hunter coughed. "They raised me well. I never bite off more than I can chew." He gave me a sideways glance. "Almost never, anyway."

I swallowed a smirk. I hadn't expected Hunter to join in, but he did it with style.

"How can I help you guys?" She bit her lip.

"I couldn't stop gushing about how much you resemble Ariana Grande to"—I palmed Hunter's warm, strong shoulder—"my friend, and he dared me to, to . . ."

"To take a picture with you," Hunter swooped in.

"Exactly. Right." I squeezed his shoulder before releasing. "Do you mind?"

"Okay, but I'm not photogenic."

"Don't worry. Nine months working for *Scribe* and Hunter has never taken a bad picture."

I passed my phone to Hunter, who was staring at me strangely.

I slid an arm around Daisy's waist. "Mind throwing your arms around me?"

She did, and I used her movement to slip out the key card.

Hunter snapped a few photos and handed my phone back with a wry shake of his head.

I thanked her for helping me out. She laughed, coyly. "Drink something and maybe later I can help you both out again." I choked on the brazenness of the offer.

Me and my slutty ass took off at rocket speed.

Five steps into the blessedly empty union link, Hunter

snorted. "That was excellent drive-by flirting." He rolled beside me. "The way you hugged her. I almost believed you were into it."

I shrugged. "I've had a lot of practice fooling people."

"Ah. When you were with Jack?"

My stomach took a dive. "Yeah. Have I mentioned I have shit for brains?"

Hunter reached around my ass and dipped into my pocket. Slowly, he drew out the keycard. I'd feel the ghost of that touch on my ass cheek all night. "What better remedy than a library?"

"I SNAP AFTER MY SISTER?"

I pulled the two-volume 1972 graduate yearbook from the dusty floor-to-ceiling bookshelf. Heavy beasts. I'd have to come back for the others when we looked for our K. I winced. Finding a four-leaf clover might be easier.

Hunter held his cell phone, casting torch light over this nook of the library. I hugged the hefty books and observed the dark pink lines of Hunter's lips. "You have a big mouth." Said mouth stretched into a smile, and I jerked my gaze up. "It was the first thing that came to my mind."

We moved to a nearby table, moonlight shafting through stained glass and imprinting on the wooden surface. Hunter tried the lamp but it didn't switch on so he set his phone atop the lampshade. Amber light spilled over the table. A cocoon of warmth in a daunting library of darkness.

I pulled the chair to the left, leaving space for Hunter to roll next to me.

His presence at my side felt big. Cozy, but also unnerving.

Humming to myself, I scrolled painfully through headshots and captioned names, jotting down any men with the initials V.A. or three-lettered names with a V.A. combination. The brain-tiring work was made harder with Hunter tapping away on his laptop, taking my V.A. names and doing his Geek Force thing in a suave manner.

"Okay." I scribbled down another name. "That makes four."

I flipped the page and scanned it.

"Great," Hunter said, fingers braced at the edge of the desk, eyes on me. "So, I might be wrong—"

"Five!"

"—You've been humming Chopin's Funeral March."

"Yep."

"For the last half an hour."

Goosebumps skittered down my arm. "The melody feels fitting for the situation."

I met a heftily raised brow. "Is there some metaphorical death that's happened here that I don't know about?"

I leaned back in my chair. "Nah, it's a haunting piece. Suspenseful." I gestured around us. "The air feels tight."

"Tight?"

Like my skin. I shoved the first volume of graduates back and opened the second one.

"Yes," Hunter mused. "The air does have a certain tightness to it."

A panicked prickle rose up my nape. I swung back on my chair, balancing on its back legs, not looking at Hunter. "It's because we're not supposed to be here. And it's mostly dark."

"Hmm."

"Get back to cross-referencing."

He gave me a warning look. "Stop swaying on your chair. Wouldn't want you to fall."

I stopped, legs snapping to the hardwood floor.

Another ten, twenty, thirty searched pages. I side-eyed Hunter frowning at his screen. "So what made you break the rules with me?"

"I like to get my thrills where I can, and this doesn't hurt anyone."

"What other thrilling shenanigans have you gotten up to in the past?"

"Too many to recount."

"Your favorite."

"Moonlight skinny dipping in Patoka Lake, while my parents and Shannon slept in a nearby cabin."

"Daredevil. Who were you with?"

Hunter's lips twisted. "Uh, nobody. It was just . . . Me and nature and silky water caressing my bits."

"Nice."

Hunter smiled fondly. "It was."

I nudged him with my elbow. "So . . . an ex-boyfriend, then?"

He smirked. "My first."

"So was this . . . I mean, time wise . . . Was it . . ."

"Before?" Hunter said, patting his thighs. "By a few months."

A cold ache pounded in my head and sternum. I imagined Hunter lazily swimming about, imagining his future and having no idea how his life would change in a few months. I swallowed. God, how did this happen?

No one at the *Scribe* ever talked about it. All I knew was Hunter was paralyzed from the waist down.

I bit my lip on asking. I wanted to know, but those questions were intensely personal—and fuck, I needed to look away from his chair.

I buried my concentration in searching for another V.A. in the yearbook

We kept glancing sideways, never quite pinning the other in the act. Like a game of tag, and I was petrified of being "it."

After twenty skin-tingling minutes, I slapped the yearbook shut. "That's it. Five."

Hunter clacked on his keyboard.

I peered at his screen. "Done your bit yet?"

"Almost."

"I'll search other yearbooks for K's."

Hunter grimaced. "Arduous task."

Arduous, all right. After an hour, and more than forty K's listed, I slammed the 1974 yearbook shut. Done searching for K's, done wondering about their fate. Done fearing how their romance had played out. "I bet we'll find both guys and they'll be alive. But V never forgave K."

Hunter paused, fingers hovering over the keyboard. "Why do you bet that?"

"Because." I shrugged. "So you bet they're together?"

Hunter's shoulders slumped. "I wish."

"But you don't believe it either." I finished for him. I balanced on the back chair legs, a rotten stodginess in my gut. "Let's get out of here—"

My chair swung too far back and I felt the rush of gravity begin to punish me. "Fuck."

I didn't fall.

Hunter reflexively clasped my shoulder and steered me and my chair upright. My feet found relieving purchase on the ground.

I let out a barely audible "thanks."

His hand dragged down my arm, resting at the back of my wrist. Calloused fingers lightly pressing into my skin.

With his other hand, he hit the Enter key. "Got it. Three of our five V.A's were drafted."

I stared at his fingers on me, arm frozen underneath. "Excellent. We'll return the keycard and that's us done for the night."

Hunter squeezed my wrist and let go. "We'll return the keycard. But we are not done for the night."

"We're not?"

He looked at me, contemplative. "Can I give you a lift home?"

My stomach hopped. "A lift?"

"A ride in my van to your current abode."

I rolled my eyes, bit my lip, and answered.

Hunter careened around corners and I clutched the overhead handle like my life depended on it. Which maybe it did.

"Holy shit. *Slow down.*"

Hunter slanted me a baffled look. "Huh?"

"You drive like a madman."

"Hey, I drive super well."

"Well enough to *kill*."

Hunter laughed and lessened his grip on the gas. A little. "No one has told me I'm a shit driver before."

"I didn't say shit. Shit would be an improvement on this. You drive like there's no tomorrow."

"That's the only way to live. Life's short."

"Well," I said pointedly, glaring at the amber light he ran through. "It will be."

"Okay, okay. I hear you."

His driving slowed, and he even deigned to use the blinker.

"Thanks, though," I said. "For driving me."

"Thank you for not taking up Daisy's offer to get lucky."

"Why, would you have gone for it?"

Hunter hesitated. "I might have been tempted. But I'm not particularly into threesomes."

"You know this from experience?"

"Yes."

I stroked my jaw. Definitely due for a shave tomorrow. "You're welcome then, I guess." I jerked a finger toward the left. "You passed my street."

"I know." Hunter looked at me. "We haven't finished talking."

"Oh, I'm pretty much done."

Hunter smirked. "You are boiling with questions. You have been the whole night. Don't think I haven't noticed you staring at my lap." His voice lowered and his gaze locked onto mine. "Don't think I didn't read through your nervous humming of Chopin's Funeral March."

"The air was tight!"

"With curiosity and unasked questions!"

Heat flared on my cheeks and I was grateful for the darkness. Fuck.

"It's okay, Marc. You can ask me."

I glanced at his lap again. I couldn't help it.

Hunter spoke gently, "I used to have a leg bag, now I use an intermittent catheter. I drain my bladder every four to six hours depending a bit on how much I've drunk."

"Oh, um . . ."

"For . . . other stuff, I have a morning routine with a little chemical assistance. Accidents occasionally happen. It sucks, but I deal with it."

I nodded, fascinated. Still fighting questions on the tip of my tongue. I tried to keep cool, but my curiosity gleamed through my hands repetitively rubbing my thighs.

"As for my junk, I can still get hard. Not from thoughts alone, but manual stimulation. Viagra."

The heels of my hands paused mid-thigh, digging in. Images flashed in my mind of Hunter fucking guys, getting fucked, and—

Wow, it was hot in here.

"I don't feel orgasms in the base of my balls and cock. Since this"—he gestured to his legs—"other parts of my body have become more sensitive. Like a fuck-ton more sensitive."

I cracked open the window an inch, sucking in the cooler night air.

"My nipples might as well be two miniature dicks for how good they can make me feel. And my neck, below my left ear . . ." Hunter blew out a breath, and I sucked one in to steady the thundering beat of arousal in my veins.

Hunter observed me. "Too much information?"

I jerked a finger at my hard crotch. "Too much information?"

Hunter grinned; I casually flipped him off—in a light-hearted way, not like in the past—and he laughed.

We drove around the block, and once again Hunter passed my street. "What now?"

"You keep opening and shutting your mouth like a goddamn fish. Ask me already."

I scowled at him. "Fine. How did you end up without the use of your legs?"

"Ah." Hunter's expression turned somber as he weighed how best to answer. Or if he *should* answer?

"Forget it. It's too personal."

Hunter gestured toward my dick, which had thankfully settled down. "I think we've well and truly crossed into the personal." He shrugged. "We might have crossed that earlier in the summer, Fawkes."

The reminder of our online conversations struck a weird bolt of electricity through me, along with the urge to read over all our past chats.

"I was seventeen."

"How old are you now?"

"Twenty-two."

I nodded, nervously folding my arms.

"There's no way to sugar-glaze the story. Some guy beat me up with a baseball bat after basketball practice. Maybe he saw me with my boyfriend, god knows we didn't hide our relationship. I won't ever know why for certain. They never caught him."

I stared out the windshield at the broken white center lines blurring by. Cool air swirled through the window, but it had little to do with the cold I felt in my chest.

Hunter continued, "The bat caught me in my spine and paralyzed me from the waist down. One single stroke."

My throat clamped.

"But I had the best care, a wonderful physiotherapist, and a life-saving therapist. I have basketball and good friends, and I don't let this stop me from doing anything I want."

An angry shudder rolled through me. "I'm . . . Oh, fuck. Stop the car."

Hunter frowned. "You okay?"

I blinked back the heat in my eyes. My voice sounded wispy. "I gotta . . . Stop the car."

Hunter halted at the sidewalk, van still humming. "Marc, would you look at me?"

"I can't." I fumbled for the door handle. "I'm sorry for . . . Fuck, everything. See you around."

I lurched out of the van, much like my insides lurched to my mouth. We were two streets from my place, and I shivered as I raced to Uncle Ben's brick bungalow.

My phone buzzed in my pocket. Once. Twice. Three times.

I hurried inside and dry retched, bowed over the toilet.

My phone rang.

I drew it out. Hunter, of course. I wanted to answer—to hear his voice—but I didn't.

My stomach flipped again.

I slumped against the sink and avoided my reflection in the mirror.

A hefty bang rattled the back door and I jumped. Hunter's voice followed, demanding I open the door.

Fuck. Uncle Ben was sleeping.

I opened the door reluctantly and a glowering Hunter rolled inside with hard jerks on his wheels.

When I shut the door, he spoke. "What the actual hell?"

His eyes pierced mine and I folded my arms, shifting my stare, teeth gritted. "Yeah, I know. I needed fresh air."

"Sure," came the sarcastic response.

"I'm . . . I didn't expect it."

Hunter sighed and his glare softened. "Okay."

"I'm sorry you had to chase after me."

"It's certainly been a thrilling evening."

A strangled laugh. Coming from me, apparently.

Hunter slung onto the couch, shifted his chair, and beckoned me over. Deja vu. "Tell me what's got you upset."

"I mean," I said, forcing up a wry smile, "It's an upsetting story."

"Yeah, but there's more to your reaction."

"How do you know?"

"Sit down?"

I sank onto the cushion next to him, eyes riveted away from his . . .

"There," I said. "Sitting."

Hunter stretched an arm on the back of the couch behind me. "Anything we can work out?"

I hiccupped. Dammit.

Hunter's fingers brushed my back, perhaps the same part of the spinal cord that he'd had bashed.

My throat jutted with a swallow.

"What's going on, Marc?"

Marc. Again, said so softly.

My voice came out strained, which was better than letting the sob free. "No one ever talks about it, so I didn't . . . I mean, you make up scenarios in your head, don't you?" I glanced at Hunter. "Tonight, before . . . I would've bet it happened in a car accident."

Hunter chuckled abruptly. "Will you ever hop in the van with me again?"

"Probably not." We shared a fleeting smile—the barest of reprieves—and then I looked away. "A car accident would have been tragic. But there are other ways it could have happened, and, of course, once or twice, you think of something worse. Something intentionally violent and horrifying. But you shove that thought away, because it's the worst one. The one that is never allowed to have happened."

Hunter nods. "And that was what happened."

My voice broke with anger. "Someone like Jack did this to you. Someone like the guy I hung out with and never said no to.

Someone I stupidly crushed on. That's the character I deemed my friend, that I *jerked off* to."

Hunter settled a warm hand on my nape and gently massaged.

"Someone who could do terrible things to a beautiful person. I'm so fucking upset, Hunter, I can't even grapple with it."

His fingers dragged up to the base of my hair and he was murmuring "it'll be all right."

I jerked out of his reach. "It is not all right. You will never be . . ."

"Who knows. Maybe science has a breakthrough and I'll be running marathons in ten years."

I stared at him, awed. Alarmed. "How are you so calm? How are you always so unbelievably content with everything?"

Hunter tugged my arm, urging me to lean into him. I wanted to, badly, but frustration had me shaking him off.

He sighed. "I'm not always okay."

"Ha!"

"You bullshit your way through life a lot, too, Marc."

I stiffened. "Too?"

"Maybe I recognize it for a reason."

I scrubbed my face and blew out a hard breath. "Fuuuuuck."

"No longer in the mood," Hunter said. "Grab your laptop."

I spared him a quizzical look, and Hunter pulled out his laptop. "Let's play a round of Demon-Slayage."

We played next to one another, and it was awkward, and . . . distracting. I was no good as a knight all summer, and I wasn't any better now. And yet . . .

Fawkes stayed at DaMage's side as we set out on a mission to find an enchanted shield that protected the wearer from most demons.

Hunter and I didn't speak. But we didn't give up the hunt until we found the shield.

I couldn't believe that after my shit-ass reaction to his intensely personal story, he stayed by my side.

CHAPTER SIX

Half a week passed, and I spent all of it wondering what Hunter was doing.

He'd stayed until two a.m. on Friday night and I had barely heard from him since. He was out of state until Thursday at a basketball tourney. Not that life revolved around Hunter.

But . . . we had a gazebo to save, and there was an alumni event tonight that might offer insight. Perhaps old photos could provide a clue, or someone who knew the lovers, or better yet, V and K themselves.

By Thursday dinner, I'd thoroughly cleaned my basement, thrown out all old sweatpants, gone for the first run in months, showered and shaved, and checked my phone for messages three times. He should be back in town by now.

"Uh oh, I hope dinner isn't disturbing all those thoughts."

I snapped my gaze from my plate of mashed potatoes and chicken to Uncle Ben. "Huh?"

"Oh good, you're still amongst the land of the mentally conscious."

"I was daydreaming."

"Would this have anything to do with Mr. Hunter?"

"No! Why would you say that?"

"That panicked answer and your earlier quivering smile. I doubt my potatoes elicited such fondness."

"Piss off."

"Watch your tongue, Mr. Jillson. I speak it how I see it."

Grumbling, I shoved a hand through my hair. "He and I are working on saving Lover's Loop gazebo. That's all."

"And Elton John only produced one hit."

I prodded my chicken. "God, imagine if you could only pick one—which one would you pick?" Hands down: *Sorry Seems to be the Hardest Word.* I tossed Uncle Ben a challenging smirk. "'Saturday Night's Alright for Fighting.' Or Thursday, in this case."

He stroked his beard, shrewdly eying me. "'Can You Feel The Love Tonight?' Stop changing the subject."

"Stop assuming how things are with Hunter and me."

Uncle Ben grimaced and conceded with a nod. "Tell me about your plan to save the gazebo."

I told him our plan.

"It'll make a good story. You might be able to claim some historic value, but most likely your biggest power is in exploiting its sentimental value. Stir up emotions."

"How do we do that?"

"Keep researching your lost letters story, it sounds powerful. Uncover more."

"More stories? Love stories?" I hummed it over. "The gazebo *is* covered in padlocks and initials."

Uncle Ben smiled. "Including my own . . ."

Uncle Ben's story made me feel . . . things. Things that weren't doing my belly any good.

I went back in the basement and distracted myself, poring

over K's letters again. His guilt and remorse were palpable. Or maybe it only felt that way because it triggered my own.

That thought was how I ended up bowed over my desk, penning my own apologies to everyone I'd wronged. Amongst them a letter for Tyler and Uncle Ben, and the one I struggled writing most: Liam's. I rewrote his three times, unable to capture how sorry I was that I habitually hurt his feelings by claiming he had none.

I simmered in shame before stowing the letters into a folder. Writing them was one thing. Actually handing them to anyone was another game altogether.

With curiosity and boredom as a motivator, I opened the Demon-Slayage chat archives and clicked on a random date earlier in the summer.

July 24

DaMage: Dinner is Fettuccine al Pomodoro with a sprig of basil.

Me: Cool. I'm eating takeout.

DaMage: Careful there, I might fall asleep from the overabundance of details.

Me: It tastes good.

DaMage: Tut-tut. Never any glimpse into the man behind Fawkes.

Me: Wouldn't want to ruin the mystery.

DaMage: Can't have a mystery without clues . . .

Me: And red herrings.

DaMage: Oh, you veil enough facts from me. I'm sure of it.

Me: . . .

Me: I'm a male student in my third year of university.

DaMage: That really narrows things down.

Me: My favorite fantasy movie is *Jumanji*.

DaMage: Okay, you got me there. Last admission I expected. Which version?

Me: Robin Williams'.

DaMage: What about LOTR?

Me: Nope, *Jumanji*.

DaMage: But . . . Why?

Me: Do you want to spend all night chatting about me? Or kick some demon ass?

DaMage: . . .

His non-committal response gave me a nervous tickle.

I scrolled down the chat, through tactical suggestions to the end.

Me: You're a fucking brilliant mage. Why are you hitching your star to my knight?

DaMage: Why *Jumanji?*

Me: It was the last movie mom and I watched together before she died of a stroke.

DaMage: God, Fawkes. I'm sorry I pressed.

Me: Your turn.

DaMage: Sure you want me to ruin the mystery?

Me: Time's ticking.

DaMage: It's simple.

DaMage: I write to you, and you write back.

I swallowed a lump in my throat and fished my phone from my pocket. I juiced it in my palm for a few minutes, before mumbling, "Fuck it."
I spun off a text.

Me: Want to crash an alumni party with me?

An answer came almost immediately. Had Hunter been staring at his phone, too?

Hunter: Let me slip into a tux. If we do this, we do it right.

I smirked.

Me: Bring a corsage.

Hunter: You'll let me pick you up and drive you?

Me: Don't you know? I'm all about second chances.

BLACK SUIT. Teeth brushed. Phone in pocket.

I straightened the collar and slipped into dress shoes.

Pretty decent. My sandy bangs were behaving for once. Pity nothing could be done for the arrogant tilt of my nose.

I jogged upstairs for my uncle's good opinion. His jaw unlocking and hanging open was judgment enough. "Next you'll be telling me you're ready to move out."

"You clearly haven't seen the state of my bank account."

I told him not to wait up—like he would—and enjoy *Downton Abbey* for the fifth time, earning me a sofa cushion to the head.

Still chuckling, I answered the knock at my basement door.

Hunter.

My gaze ping-ponged as I took all of him in. His hair was neatly coiffured, his dress shoes gleamed, the gray suit fit perfectly, and the white shirt under his jacket shone like it was newly bought. Maybe it was. Or maybe Hunter took better care of his shit. His wheelchair was different too, fancier—he'd used sleek spoke guards to accessorize.

Hunter rolled back and scrolled a slow gaze from my head to my toe, lips curling.

"Did you just check me out?"

"Yes." He curled a finger for me to come closer, and I did, as if pulled by an invisible cord. An invisible cord shooting electricity from my hands to my feet to the base of my balls. He snagged my tie and used it to pull me down. "Not for the first time, either."

Our faces were an inch apart and I braced my damp palms on his chair.

His fingers picked up an object from inside the chair and tugged my left breast pocket.

"What do you think?" Hunter said.

"About your eyes lingering on my crotch?"

"About the boutonniere." He winked, dropping his fingers from me. "I already know what you think about my eyes lingering on your crotch."

I flustered and stood upright. A light red carnation. I hadn't been serious about Hunter bringing me a corsage. Or a boutonniere.

My cheeks burned holding the freaking smile on my face. "I wasn't serious about bringing one of these."

"You weren't, maybe. I am."

From above, a third voice cut in. Uncle Ben called from the window. "I'm not assuming anything."

"Good," I called up to him.

"Now I'm deducing."

I gestured to Hunter we leave. "How was basketball?"

"It was a good week. Made semis. What was happening with the Chief?" Hunter deftly shifted into the driver's seat and swung his wheelchair into the back via the sliding door.

"Uncle Ben?" I nervously clipped in my belt. "Oh, he's old."

"Old? Looks fit to me. Not far past forty."

"Forty-three. But he doesn't understand that guys can flirt without it meaning anything."

It was the wrong thing to say.

It was a *stupid* thing to say.

Silence descended between us as we drove.

"Uncle Ben is rooting for us to save the gazebo too," I tossed out, hoping for a reaction, almost sighing when Hunter raised a quizzical brow.

"Yep," I said. "His initials are carved into it."

"I thought he was single."

"He is. But he and his best friend used to be lovers. They're still crazy close despite the distance."

"Distance?"

"Jason was an international ballet dancer, and now he travels as a trainer. He comes to Pittsburgh twice a year, and I'm realizing that maybe it's not as over as Uncle Ben claimed. Maybe Jason is why he never dates."

I rubbed my chest, feeling a soft ache.

"What's their origin story?" Hunter queried.

I smirked, recalling Uncle Ben's description. "Wasted out of his mind, he entered the wrong dorm room—a floor below his own—and climbed into Jason's bed. When he woke up in the morning, Jason was staring at him. Uncle Ben gaped back, transfixed by his beauty, and said: *Oh wow, that must have been a good night.* Jason bust out a laugh and has been laughing at him ever since."

"And the gazebo?"

"Gayzebo, I'm starting to think."

Hunter snorted and rolled his eyes. "How does that fit in?"

"Uncle Ben was embarrassed after his bed-nabbing escapade so he evaded Jason. Said he had never seen Jason before that morning, yet suddenly he was everywhere."

"Funny how that happens."

"Uncle Ben's a big guy. Played varsity football. He sprained his foot jumping behind the bushes trying to hide from Jason. Jason had to haul him out and act as a crutch to the gazebo."

"See, stories like these make me *need* to save the gazebo."

"He wants me to write his story for the next *Scribe* issue."

"I can't wait to read it." Hunter gently halted at an amber light and peered at me.

"What?"

"When did you move into Chief Benedict's basement?"

Ugh. Heaviness settled on my shoulders and sank to my toes. I laughed, but it sounded tinny to my ears. "As soon as dad could get me off his hands. Sixteen, just."

The light turned green, but Hunter didn't drive. The dead side street didn't allow for rude beeping, so nothing broke Hunter's sympathetic gaze. I pulled my focus to the street.

"Listen, I don't deserve the pity. I was a shit teenager. I made it real tough, I'm surprised he didn't leave earlier."

"Marc——"

"Now the light's red again."

"*Marc.*"

He wanted me to look at him, but I couldn't lift my chin. "You know, maybe Uncle Ben and Jason aren't together because I crashed into his life six years ago and crimped his ability to travel around the world and live out of a suitcase alongside his love." I shoved down those shameful memories and leaned against the headrest. "Well, fuck. There's definitely no making it up to him."

"Marc, you are too hard on yourself. You were a kid, you deserved someone looking after you." Hunter rubbed his jaw, and added, "I've always respected Chief Benedict, but now I might be a little in love with him."

"You and my uncle . . ." I turned my horrified gaze on him. "You're great at making a guy feel better."

Hunter threw back his head, laughed, and took the next green.

WE PARKED close to Ronald Hall. I'd been here a few times; it housed campus assemblies, celebrations, fundraisers.

"So," I said, awkwardly, wondering how much I could ask, "When did you get in today?"

"Afternoon. Liam and I hit the market, and Quinn used our produce to cook dinner."

"What are they up to tonight?"

Hunter turned off the engine. "Tantric sex, Liam hopes."

I choked on an inhale. "You're joking."

"Something you learn about Liam: He never jokes."

"Seriously, he tells you that stuff?"

Hunter cracked open his door and opened the sliding door. "It's sex, Marc. We don't have to be secretive about it."

"I don't know. Feels kinda personal."

He reached behind him, pulled his chair out, and transferred into it. He stared at me still buckled into the passenger seat. "Guess that depends on who you're doing it with."

I scrambled out of the van and followed him across the dark street to the warmly lit hall. Did that mean he practiced a lot of impersonal sex?

I felt a stomach-twisting emotion between jealousy and sadness. Something to delve into later, maybe. Rolling through the entrance of the old hall, we ran into a line of people searching for their names among the two dozen leftover tags. A rotund woman —mid-fifties, with a bored expression—sat on the other side, nodding at guests.

One look at the alumni surrounding us, and there was a hitch in our plans.

Hunter caught on. "Maybe if you didn't shave tonight, entrance would be easier."

"You think a little scruff ages me twenty years?" I rubbed my palms together. "Follow my lead. If we don't get in, it's because we didn't bullshit hard enough."

"I'm not sure if I'm rooting for us to get in or get caught."

"Hey, you said you fake it too."

"I didn't say I was proud of it."

"Well, I don't see how else we'll get in."

"What if we tell her the truth? She's bound to let in a *Scribe* reporter and photographer."

"Without his camera? Let's say she doesn't, what then?"

"We have two V.A. names, and I hacked around and got their addresses. Both alive and kicking. We can do door-to-door service tomorrow."

"Two? I thought we had three?"

"The eye color of one didn't match, leaving two brown-eyed V.A.'s."

I pivoted, legs in front of his chair, and eyed him closely. Hunter locked his eyes onto mine for a heart-quickening beat. "If you've narrowed it down this far," I asked slowly, "why did you agree to come here tonight?"

He dropped his gaze to the carnation, and my heart rattled around behind it.

He turned his head toward the doors, a flash of vulnerability and disappointment creasing his brow, quickly masked. "Maybe I didn't think things through."

I write to you, and you write back.

I sucked in a rain-laced breath. His sister was away, Liam was busy loving Quinn . . . Maybe he was always on Demon-Slayage for the same reason I was.

Carefully, I said, "Getting in will be another thrill." I winked at him. "I like getting my thrills with you."

I thought it might make Hunter smile, but instead it deepened his frown.

In the end, entrance was easy. Our hostess retreated for the ladies' room, and I didn't waste a second penning names onto two blank nametags.

We entered the bigger of two adjacent rooms, where all the movement and laughter stemmed from. Guests carried on jolly conversations around tall, chairless, disabled-unfriendly tables. Ahead, on stage, a podium under a *Welcome Alumni* banner.

Waiters offered guests flutes of champagne or tumblers of juice. I grabbed two flutes and handed one to Hunter.

We tossed them back fairly quickly and grabbed refills. Champagne for me, juice for Hunter.

A familiar, rather puzzled "hello" surprised us from behind. Hannah stood in a slinky black dress and bright red lipstick, hair pinned elegantly. "Hannah!"

Hunter turned around too, draining his juice. He beckoned a passing waiter and ended up with a fresh drink.

"What are you guys doing here?" Hannah glanced at our nametags. "Dick Longe? William Stroker?"

I smirked. "You can call him Willie."

Hunter read his name tag and shook his head.

"What?" I said. "Dick and Willie are classic old guy names. We fit right in here."

Hannah's expression pinched. "Stop being a jackass."

Jackass. Jack. Ass.

You are just like me.

I stared at my champagne.

"What are you doing here?" Hunter asked Hannah politely, while I stewed in stupidity.

Hannah glanced around the room. "My great uncle is hiding around here somewhere—and it's also my party page article for the next issue."

An excited voice vibrated through the on-stage microphone, silencing the guests.

". . . a wonderful evening. Please give a big welcome to the great-grandson of Gable University founder, and graduate of 1974: Kyle Gable Green."

Hunter and I looked at each other sideways, and in comical timing, both said, "Kyle Gable Green?"

Hannah giggled. "Pretty hot for a seventy-year-old, huh?"

Sure, the guy kept in shape, had a strong jawline, a healthy crop of silver hair, and a keen gaze.

"Seriously," Hannah said. "Why are you here? And together? Did the Chief put you onto this without telling me?"

I shook my head. "Nothing like that. I'm following a lead on our gazebo story."

"Ah, okay. You're here for the photos."

I had no idea what she was talking about, but nodded anyway. "Someone is waving at you," I lied, glancing over her shoulder.

Hannah excused herself to scuttle off in that direction. Hopefully I didn't send her on a complete goose chase. But I needed a moment with Hunter.

"Kyle Gable Green?" I said expectantly. "Could he be our K?"

"Maybe."

Holy shit. That added a whole new level of difficulty to V and K's relationship. The Gables had been prominent city figures for generations. Alongside Gable University, they founded a private hospital, and held a huge stake in the steel industry.

Hunter and I stared at each other, bewildered.

Could it really be K? I whipped out my phone and googled Kyle Gable Green. Studied at Gable University from 1969-1974, graduating with a double master's in business and humanities.

"He studied around the right time."

Hunter glanced up from his phone. "And never went to war."

Kyle took the podium. "On my way here tonight, my great niece gave me tips on my speech. She said, don't try to dazzle them with charm, spout anything philosophical or intellectual, and don't whip out the witty jokes. Just be yourself."

The crowd chuckled.

"And she is right. Being true to yourself, no matter the obstacle . . . that is true courage."

I knew in my gut this was our author. Not only had he started with a joke, like so many of K's letters, I'd read those exact words on being true to yourself in there too.

"It's him," I said.

Hunter nodded. "Guess coming here was worthwhile after all."

Kyle's speech faded into the background as I looked at Hunter and his matching carnation. "It would have been worthwhile either way," I murmured.

Hunter's head tilted, and I pivoted toward the stage. Kyle spoke in a deep, husky timbre, constantly scanning the crowd. He paused for an awkward beat before continuing with a sad little smile. "After the varsity acapella choir performs, we'll open the gallery."

"There's a gallery?" That was what Hannah had meant by photos. I perked up. "Maybe there's a picture of the gazebo? Or something with K and V in it? Let's look."

"He said after the choir—"

"I know a side entrance."

"Of course you do."

I grabbed another flute of champagne and led the way, ploughing into a gentleman with a tiger-headed cane emerging from the gallery. Someone else had the sneaky idea to have an early peek. "Sorry, sir."

The silver-haired man tipped his chin and caned off.

Hunter lifted a brow. "Sorry, sir? I didn't know you could pull off polite."

I shrugged. "Guess it's part of the act."

Hunter shook his head, and I opened the narrow door leading into the gallery. The air hummed with the opening harmony of "Somebody to Love," and the voices vibrated through my champagne flute as I followed Hunter inside.

Bright overhead lights showcased hundreds of framed photos. Hunter rolled quietly beside me and caught me watching him.

"Why'd you do it?" he asked, touching the edges of his Willie Stroker nametag.

I shrugged. Champagne bubbles were *fascinating*.

He stopped moving and so did I. "Were you trying—and failing—to be funny?"

I glared at him, exasperated. Guilty. "I was trying—and failing—to make you smile."

He stilled, brow pinching, the line of his mouth softening.

"It's not the only stupid thing I've done tonight." I laughed tightly over the sharp regret of telling him I was flirting without it meaning anything. "You should reconsider hanging out with me."

Clutching my flute, I swiveled to the nearest wall of pictures. Hunter moved to the opposite wall.

Some pictures were set too high, and I hated that lack of foresight.

I found one picture of the gazebo with two fuzzy figures seated in the shadows. Pity the details were impossible to make out. The caption simply read *Lover's Loop gazebo*. Adjacent was a picture of a young, determined Kyle Gable Green playing baseball, bat at the ready. Fingerprints smudged the glass, but his face was still recognizable as the older man onstage. At the corner of the picture, an autograph. K.

The K scrawled in the same loopy way as our—no longer anonymous—author.

Staring at the young man and having such an insight into his life at the time was surreal. I checked the date. Before the draft. After he'd met V. Had Kyle finished that game, found V, and made love to him that night? Had they laughed and bantered, and dreamed of their future together?

A frustrated grunt carried over the room. Hunter cursed, head bowed toward his lap.

"You okay?" I asked.

He spun off another "fuck", and his back stiffened as I neared him.

I realized his predicament as soon as I stepped to his side. My fingers tightened on my flute glass.

A wet patch stained Hunter's gray suit pants.

He struggled to lift his head and look at me. His cheeks were flushed red, his jaw tight. "I fucked up my timing."

I shifted from foot to foot, equally flushed. "Well, I mean . . ." I wanted him to know it didn't matter, that I didn't care.

The doors beside us opened wide. An anticipative alumni crowd gathered behind Kyle. I felt the wattage of Hunter's blazing embarrassment.

I didn't waste one second. I tipped the contents of my flute on Hunter's crotch to the sharp gasp of onlookers.

"You don't want me?" I yelled at him. "Good luck anyone wanting *you* tonight."

For a second, I wasn't sure he understood. But I followed through on my act and stormed out of the room across the puddled street to Hunter's van, the crowd parting with disgusted hisses. I wondered ashamedly if Hannah had witnessed the fight and if she'd ever forgive me. I leaned against his driver's door and eyed the entrance.

Hunter wasn't far behind. A minute or two, no more.

I imagined people would have fawned over him, asking if he was okay, if they could help. Hunter would politely decline, because he could handle everything himself.

I smiled at that thought. How fucking strong Hunter was.

As if proving my point, he rolled across the road, chin high. He unlocked the van and the sliding door opened automatically. I pressed my back against the cold driver's side and stared at the puddle-filled potholes that reflected the streetlights. I felt him watching me but wanted to give him privacy.

He transferred himself into the back of the van.

"I have a change of clothes back here," he said.

"Cool. Yeah. Take your time."

"The front's open, if you want to get in."

I got in, snapping the belt on. Hunter shifted around in the back.

"Our K offered to help me," Hunter said.

"Oh, right."

"I said I was from *Scribe*, that I wanted an interview."

"You did?"

"He's away on business next week, but he gave me this." I took the lime-colored card Hunter offered. "We can call and set up a date for the following week."

I stared at the card. Nodded. "Are we really going door-to-door tomorrow?"

Hunter made a series of sounds in the back. A shuffle, a zip puttering open, a rustle, a long hum. "I have so much work to catch up on, *Scribe* and a home basketball game tomorrow, I don't think I can swing it until Saturday."

I nodded, not that he would necessarily see me. I mean, he could look my way. I just couldn't look his.

I mean, I technically could, but . . . privacy. "Probably more likely to be at home on Saturday, right?"

Hunter moved into the driver's seat and slung his wheelchair into the back. The doors shut, and freshly changed and flushed, Hunter looked at me. "You good?"

"Like in general, or with our plans?"

"Both. Our plans."

"I'm good. As long as you invite me to your game."

Hunter did a double take. His hands shifted on the steering wheel. "You want to come?"

"I definitely want to be invited."

Hunter laughed, and relief washed through me. "Squirrel Hill sport center. Six p.m."

"If it helps the studying, I typed notes for your missed classes."

"You did?"

I shrugged. "Figured I owed you."

With a soft grin, he started the van and we drove to my place. We chatted about the news and the idiocy of the world. The conversation could have spiraled on forever.

He parked outside the bungalow and the radio cut out. Silence was thick and heavy.

"So, yeah . . ." I said, unbuckling.

Hunter looked at me, considering, soft. "Thank you, Marc."

"Sure."

"I don't just mean for the notes."

I nodded.

He opened his seat belt. "Marc?"

"Yeah?"

His hands locked onto my shoulders, sure and firm. A rush of giddiness stole my breath and I yielded, folding toward him.

His warm breath slipped over my nose, my jaw. His quiet expression surged into me full of gentleness and warmth and wanting.

I trembled as his thumbs rubbed reassuring circles up my neck. He leaned in, tips of his thumbs under my ears, fingers curling around my nape, and he kissed me.

Just the brush of his lips. Then he pulled back, met my eyes, and kissed me again.

The moist press shot shivers through me. I insisted I kiss him back, but my brain short-circuited and all I could do was swallow the fresh taste of him.

I rubbed my mouth, pulsing from his gentle kiss. "Hmm, yeah. Okay."

A laugh bubbled out of me, verging on hysterical, and I clambered out of the car.

"Marc?" Hunter called after me, baffled.

I lifted a hand, a weird-ass acknowledging wave, because I couldn't look back.

CHAPTER SEVEN

Why couldn't I look back? Hell, why couldn't I *kiss* him back?

I placed my red carnation in a shot glass of water on my bedside table and stared at the comforting dark shape as I replayed Hunter's kiss. Fingers at my lips, then with a languid grip under tangled sheets.

Hunter had tasted so good. So fucking *wow*.

Hookup kisses were hard and emotionless, a means to an end. Never full of electricity.

Hunter's kiss had rendered me frozen. I hadn't expected it, and yet, when it happened, it was all I wanted. Those strong hands on my shoulders, that wide mouth slanted across mine, the heat of his breath slipping over my lips like a whisper for me to let him in.

My lips parted with a groan, like they should have in the moment. Not hours too late.

I stroked furiously, breath rough and lonely in the silence of the basement.

God, would Hunter let me . . . Hell, I really wanted to . . .

I whined out a curse and wet heat shot over my belly.

I slumped back, throwing the crook of my arm over my face. Not the first time I'd jerked off thinking about Hunter. Throughout the summer, I'd pictured his DaMage avatar and mine going at it. I never felt weird about it before, so why did I feel on edge tonight?

Because it was closer to something attainable?

Because, somewhere in the city, Hunter was sleeping with the taste of me on his lips?

Or maybe because he was frowning at his ceiling, wondering why I didn't kiss him back?

I slung out of bed and cleaned myself in the bathroom. I stared at my mussed hair and chewed lip in the mirror. "You absolute idiot."

Demon-Slayage Chat archives

July

DaMage: Fawkes, you know, I'd let a Kalvaleth demon suck the soul out of my eye socket for you. But I'd prefer to eat demon dung than follow you into that cave again.

Me: But . . . The last crystal for the potion to make me a better knight . . .

DaMage: Maybe learn to improve yourself with what you already have?

Me: I'll give you half the crystal.

DaMage: I'd prefer to strip and hula-hoop in a vampire lair than follow you into that cave again.

Me: *sigh*

DaMage: Prefer to moisturize my rosy cheeks with goblin come.

Me: Right.

DaMage: Prefer to have an incubus demon pound into me for eternity.

Me: I got it.

Me: Wait, is that last one bad?

DaMage: I suppose it depends on the incubus.

DaMage: I'd prefer to have an incubus demon pound into my throat with a spiked, hockey-stick penis than walk into that cave.

Me: Are you gonna keep this up all night?

DaMage: I'd prefer a nine-foot alpha wolf ass-impregnate me.

Demon-Slayage Chat archives

August

Me: It's a witch's cottage!

DaMage: She's dead.

Me: We're here to lay low, not play house.

DaMage: I'm just watering the herbs.

Me: Which is costing you your limited water supply. I'd prefer you alive over some plants.

DaMage: Some of these herbs could be used to save us later. The pecigella gives the consumer strength—especially knights.

Me: I won't need to be strong if you're gone. Won't need to be here at all.

DaMage: I like you too, Fawkes.

Demon-Slayage Chat archives

August

Me: Is it DaMage like Da Man? Because basically this whole time, I'm singing Da Maaaage in my head.

Me: Are you there?

Me: Nevermind.

Demon-Slayage Chat archives

August

DaMage: Short sesh today. Got a date.

Me: A date?

DaMage: Cute guy ran into me and wants to make it up over dinner. I said yes.

Me: Er . . . Have fun.

Demon-Slayage Chat archives

August

Me: Are you always going to fire spells before I can draw my knife?

DaMage: Huh?

Me: That vampire was about to suck *my* throat, and you killed him.

DaMage: And?

Me: Fine, sure. Always be the hero.

DaMage: Look, I'm sorry.

Me: Yeah, sure. Maybe ask me next time first.

DaMage: I did save your life. You're welcome.

Me: It's my life.

DaMage: What's going on, Fawkes?

Me: You blasted that thing to smithereens.

DaMage: Not the game. What's up?

Me: Why, want to save me in RL too?

DaMage: Look, right now you're being an ass.

Me: That's so not true.

DaMage: Go make yourself a drink. Jerk off. I'll chat with you later.

Demon-Slayage Chat archives

August

Me: Soooo. I'm crap at apologies.

DaMage: Acknowledgment is a start.

Me: I was upset and stupid and . . . feeling sorry for myself.

DaMage: We all have our moments.

Me: Anyway, how did your date go?

DaMage: Hmm?

Me: The one from the other day?

DaMage: Oh. He just wanted to hook up.

Demon-Slayage Chat archives

September

Me: What are you up to?

DaMage: In the game? Or RL?

Me: Wasn't talking about the game.

DaMage: My sister's leaving for a semester overseas. I'm making a goodbye dinner.

Me: Nice. Are you two close?

DaMage: We used to be, and I think we will be again.

Me: But not right now?

DaMage: She's been a bit overprotective of me.

Me: Overprotective?

DaMage: Older sibling.

Me: Oh, right. I wouldn't know. Only child. AKA spoiled brat.

DaMage: Or ultra-independent? What are you up to?

Me: My uncle's best friend is staying the week. I'm hiding.

Me: What are you making for dinner?

DaMage: Tagliatelle con ragu bolognese

Me: Sounds delicious. Think of me when you eat it.

DaMage: Think of you?

Me: Yeah, that was weird . . .

DaMage: I do, though, think of you outside the game.

Me: I gotta . . . Sorry, Uncle Ben and Jason found me . . .

MY CHEEKS BURNED and I stopped reading through archived chats. Uncle Ben and Jason hadn't found me that night; I forced a reprieve when I could no longer stand the flurry of feelings. It was clear, in retrospect, that I'd been into Hunter for a while.

It was why finding out Hunter's true identity had been so awkward and disappointing.

Whatever friendship we'd been building up had been tainted by a real-life earlier version of me that had hurt Hunter and his friends. It was like discovering you'd planted seeds in sand instead of earth. You might have adequately watered them, but they would never grow roots.

I shut down my computer and somberly ate breakfast at the bay windows, watching Uncle Ben take off on his daily morning run. He sure had a lot of energy to burn.

Or frustration?

Sexual frustration?

Because he missed Jason, the love of his life?

I dropped my bowl into the sink with the clattering urgency to investigate. Pulse rabbiting, I snuck into Uncle Ben's home office, found his address book—a leather-bound relic—and found Jason's number.

Was I really doing this?

Yes. I needed to.

The phone rang four times before Jason picked up. "Miss me already, Harry?"

I inhaled sharply.

Jason's coy, sexy purr; the hint Uncle Ben had called recently;

and *Harry*. Uncle Benedict's given name. Something he never let anyone else use.

My heart pounded in the base of my throat.

"Harry?" Concern, tenderness.

I slammed my eyes shut. "It's not Harry."

Silence descended thickly down the line. "Marc?"

"Y-yeah."

"Shit, is Harry okay? I can fly out in three hours. Fuck, I'm hailing a cab right now—"

Jason's panic almost broke me.

"He's fine. Nothing happened to him. He doesn't know I'm calling."

Relief came in the form of a sigh and a relieved curse. And then, patiently—which is more than I might have deserved for calling like this—"Wait, why are you calling?"

"How long were you together?"

A pause. "Maybe you should speak to your uncle."

Maybe I should. "How long?"

"It's complicated."

I tossed my pen atop my notepad. "How long."

"We never stopped."

I stared at young Uncle Ben and Jason in their framed picture on the desk. "Why didn't he tell me?"

"Marc, honey, you really should talk to your uncle."

"I'm talking to you."

Jason gathered his thoughts, breathing heavily. "It's been casual the last few years."

I laughed, wryly. "The last six, you mean."

"It might have been about that."

Heat built behind my eyes and their smiling Kodak-moment blurred. "Casual meaning you're free to sleep with whoever you want while you're out of town?"

"We're mature adults, Marc."

"That's a yes, then."

"I hear that this news is upsetting you. I don't know what to say."

"I've met you, like, a dozen times over the last years. You never gave anything away."

"We were discreet."

"It's because you never liked me, right? I was a jackass, and you didn't want any part of raising that."

"Marc, listen to me. I like you."

I didn't believe him. Jason was just being a nice guy. Saying what he was meant to say.

"My passion has always been ballet. Your uncle knows that. He encourages me to live my dreams. He is the best person I know."

I blinked hard. Damp lashes coolly stamped my skin. "He never does, you know."

"Never does what?"

I stared at the ceiling, hoping it might stop the gathering tears. "Never dates."

Jason chuckled, brushing me off. "Of course he does. He dates all the time. No trouble getting lucky with a body like that!"

I shook my head. "He. Never. Dates."

Jason remained quiet.

"My uncle—"

He sucked in a sharp breath and his voice cracked. "I gotta go."

He hung up.

I dropped the phone and scrubbed my face. Fuck.

I didn't know how I could tell Uncle Ben about this call.

Or how I could make everything up to him.

But Uncle Ben and Hunter wanted to save the gazebo, and I knew I needed to make that happen.

I SPENT the rest of the day writing and rewriting my spotlight article on Uncle Ben and Jason, and devising a strategy to save the gazebo. The thing was, I needed to establish value. Not only sentimental and aesthetic, but economic.

I researched the cost of benches and pansy beds, and amateurly calculated the economic valuation of cultural heritage. I dug out my notes from Professor Shammas's class and headed to the econ department to ask for advice, calling property services on the way.

Five minutes later, I had a Tuesday meeting booked with the senior adviser overseeing the redevelopment. I texted Hunter the details, and Hunter texted back he'd be there.

I strode across the quad through a straggle of students bustling before the weekend.

Hunter: How was your day?

Just like that, his mouth was on mine. Gentle pressure at the points under my ears, the sticky heat of my nervous breath mingling with his. My veins jittered, and other places too. I bit on my smile like I could get drunk from it.

Me: It's not over yet.

After chatting with Professor Shammas, I bussed to the sports center on Squirrel Hill. I breathed in the scent of rubber, polished floor, and sweat.

The sweat was probably my own nerves.

I rolled my shoulders back and assumed a lazy swagger. Three of the five courts were in use. Judging by the uniformed guys in wheelchairs tossing balls around, one court was Hunter's.

Family, friends, and coaches gathered courtside.

Liam sat on the front bench, arm-in-arm with his tall, broad boyfriend. Quinn stared at Liam with a soft, secretive smile, while Liam gazed purposefully toward the court.

Tantric sex.

I groaned as images of entangled, sweaty limbs hijacked my mind.

I would kill Hunter for telling me that piece of information.

Hunter rolled from his teammates to Quinn. He wore a dark blue tank-top with his name printed in white. A basketball sat on his thighs. Hummingbirds covered his arms and peeked out from his tank top, and fuck it was hot in here. Seriously needed better AC.

I sat heavily on the bench.

Dimples appearing, Hunter slapped Quinn and Liam's hands. As if sensing my shameless stare, Hunter glanced along the sideline to me. He jerked with surprise, spoke to Quinn and Liam, and rolled toward me. His wheelchair was, again, different. Slanted wheels were probably better suited for sport.

"Marc." His voice sounded bright despite the undercurrent of hesitance.

I rubbed my jean-clad thighs. "Hunter."

"Just in time for the game."

"Uh huh." I nodded, watching his team high-five one another.

Hunter juggled his basketball. "Are you sure you want to be here?"

I whipped up a brow. "Yep, why not?"

"You're tapping your foot like you can't wait to bust out of here."

Liam stared blatantly in our direction. My nape felt clammy. "Well, I don't know much about wheelchair basketball, that's all."

He slanted me a look that said he knew better. "Right, wheelchair basketball."

I kept trying, arms folded, casual smile. "I thought the hoop would be lower?"

"Same rules as regular basketball. Only you bounce every two pushes of the wheel. It's okay to change your mind."

I frowned. "I haven't changed my mind."

Hunter eyed me like I was a complicated math equation. Was that the look he'd taken to bed last night? I needed to say something. Acknowledge—

"Look," Hunter said, beating me. "I'm sorry about last night. It was just a kiss."

"I mean, yeah." I shrugged off the disappointment. "No biggie."

Hunter rolled in, closer. All earnestness. "We can forget about it if you like."

I shrugged again. I was on fire in the communication department. "Sure."

He hummed, and nodded reluctantly. "If you sit next to Quinn and Liam, they'll explain anything you want to know."

I palmed my nape. Fuck, why did I come here? "I'm good right here. Great view."

Hunter pressed a sliding hand on my knee and leaned in. "If we're going to keep being friends, you'll have to talk to Liam eventually."

Talking to Liam was the last thing I wanted to do, but hearing "friends" almost had me skipping over to the guy.

I mean, I'd hoped we were friends. But hearing it was an epic relief.

I lightly punched his bicep. "Go rip up the court."

And, holy fuck, Hunter ripped up the court.

The game was ferocious. Squealing rubber and echoing bounces, testosterone-laced grunts and the delicious taste of exertion. The eye-hand coordination the team had was insane. The sweat, the glistening, flexing muscles. Hunter's total control of the ball, the easy three pointers. The heart-pounding *stamina* . . .

My stomach knotted at the tight score, and I leaped up and hollered Hunter's name when he scored the winning shot.

I wasn't the only one yelling, but I was the only one bouncing on the balls of my feet, blocking the view of the family behind me.

Hunter glanced over and winked, lips hitching lazily on one side.

I resumed my seat when my knees buckled.

The teams shook hands, and Hunter's rolled off the court for the changing rooms.

I realized most people on the sidelines knew each other. They studied me like I was the newest piece of gossip to dissect later.

That embarrassing holler would have their minds spinning.

Liam was watching me, a pensive expression on his face.

I shoved my hands into my pockets and ambled to him, each step stirring up guilt. Liam spoke to his boyfriend, who instantly scowled in my direction. Yep, this would be fun.

Liam pushed up his thick-framed glasses, and I tried to hide my awkwardness. "Liam, hey. Can we, like, talk for a moment? In private?"

Not that there was anywhere private to go. But a few steps away, just the two of us.

Liam shifted on his feet. "Anything you have to say, Quinn can hear it."

Quinn protectively folded his arms, puffed his chest out.

I admired Quinn for not letting anything happen to his Liam. "Right. I guess I wanted to apologize to you about everything last year?"

I hated my achy throat, the vagueness of my words, my faux-cavalier tone.

"That's a bit vague," Liam said. Not unkindly.

Which was more than that attempt deserved. "I mean—"

He waved me off. "Why did you hang out with Jack?"

I glanced toward the basketball hoop over his shoulder. "I didn't know he was violent."

"You knew he joked about gays."

I winced. "I thought he was in denial."

Liam laughed dryly. "Not good enough."

He turned away from me and Quinn followed his lead. My stomach lurched. If I couldn't work this out with Liam, my friendship with Hunter had an expiration date. "I crushed on him, okay?" I said, pleading. Liam paused. Faced me again.

I swallowed. "I crushed on him and wished I hadn't."

"Are you still crushing on him?"

Jack? I spat out a laugh. "No. Not him."

Liam studied me and then nodded, like this made sense. "I see why you want to make peace with me."

My fingers felt sticky in my pockets. "You're his friend. He thinks the world of you."

"And I think highly of him. So I'll say this once." He tapped my chest with his pen. "He. Deserves. Better."

Well, no denying that. "Absolutely."

Liam was taken aback. "Yes," he said, frowning.

"But pretend he wants something meaningless with me. Pretend we hang out, spend some time together. No feelings. No broken hearts. Just fun and . . . respect."

"You want to fool around with Hunter?"

I looked Liam in the eye. "Yeah, I really do."

"Why are you telling me this?"

"I just . . . You know him. He likes you. Your blessing would go a long way. Maybe you have tips about what Hunter likes, what might make a good impression. I've never met someone like him."

"Paraplegic?" Liam stiffened, Quinn too.

"Someone confident and witty and"—I grunted—"totally good. Someone who fries my insides with a single look."

I yanked my hands free from their pockets. "I guess he makes a lot of people feel like that."

I twisted and Liam's voice trailed factually after me. "He likes Peter."

I whirled back around. "Huh?"

"I mean, he loves Peter. Like, crazy loves Peter."

"Peter?" My stomach couldn't drop any lower.

"Uh huh. Ask after Peter."

Yeah. Not gonna happen.

"He also loves dancing. Going out . . ." Liam tapped his pen over his lips, thoughtfully. "We're going to a club tonight. Phoenix. Know it?"

"In Shadyside?"

"A block from Hunter's apartment."

I breathed out slowly. Hunter hadn't mentioned it, but then again, why would he invite me when he knew how awkward things were between Liam and me? "Was that an invite?"

"That was information. What you choose to do with it . . . Well." Liam shrugged and turned his attention to Quinn.

I turned my attention to forgetting my horrible attempt at apologizing, and pushing Peter out of my mind.

CHAPTER EIGHT

I was close to throwing up at the entrance to Phoenix, which I might have used as an excuse to leave if I didn't so badly want to see—kiss—Hunter again.

All my usual cool was shot. Nothing left in my bullshit reservoir to steady my thundering heart or the nervous twitch in my hands.

A group of dagger-heeled girls herded me inside, their killer shoes threatening to skewer my red Converse. A glance in the mirrored windows showed an ashen complexion under a mop of brown hair. The only thing in place was my *Talk Nerdy to Me* T-shirt.

I caught sight of Hunter laughing at a table with Liam and Quinn, and made directly—

For the bar.

I'd had two shots before taking an Uber here, and I downed another two.

Gin burned my throat as I leaned back on the bar and peered through gaps between dry-humping bodies towards a wide, laughing smile and devastating dimples.

Quinn broke from the table, parted the dance floor with his

wide shoulders and charming smirk, and ordered drinks at the bar. His gaze flowed over me and snapped back. "Jill."

I cringed but nodded. "Hey."

Quinn sidled down the bar, unsure what to think of me. He shrugged off whatever he'd been thinking. "He's using glittery spoke guards and feeling sexy tonight. Go make him swoon before someone else does."

I itched for a third shot. "Right. Okay." I clapped my hands together with purpose, pushing off the bar, and halted. "How?"

Quinn frowned. "Dance."

"Yeah, sure." I took a step in Hunter's direction, and hesitated again. "How do I . . ." I gestured toward the dry-humpers and scratched the back of my head. "Like, a lap dance?"

"Oh, Christ. You're a lost cause." Quinn took a shot and passed it to me. I slung it back with gratitude. "Just ask him," Quinn said, clapping my shoulder. "Swing him around, sing, laugh. Keep it fun. Don't ever forget you're not worthy of him."

Good to know Hunter's best friends were on the same page.

"Yeah. Haven't forgotten."

I absorbed the buzz that was growing and concentrated on the beat as I rounded writhing bodies. Hunter nursed a beer, watching couples dance. He wore jeans, silver sneakers, and a black tank top that molded to his toned chest.

Just ask him to dance. Don't, not even once, ask him who the fuck this Peter guy is.

Easy.

Hunter spotted me, and his posture straightened. He set his drink down and folded his arms. In the glittery light, his hummingbird tattoos fluttered.

I cleared my throat. "Hunter."

He rocked up a brow. "Didn't expect to see you here."

Cue a casual shrug. "Oh, if I'm not on Demon-Slayage, I'm here. I love this . . . joint."

"That right?" Hunter's lips twitched, and I couldn't look away from them.

Ask him to dance. "I met with Professor Shammas today."

"Okay." He waited for me to explain why I was really there.

"We talked about the value of conserving a cultural asset." Rivulets of sweat pearled down my pits. Dampened my nape. *Ask him to dance.* "He said we could easily argue to conserve the gazebo. Visitors benefit from it, memories are made, the gazebo may have been used in magazines and films or had virtual visitors. He said even if the gazebo isn't being used currently, that doesn't mean it won't be used more in the future."

Hunter stared at me, an amused tilt to his lips, a twinkle in his eye.

This was not going to plan.

"When assigning value to it," I continued, like an idiot, "we should consider altruistic feelings from the public as well as the conservation of a cultural landmark. If K could acknowledge the gazebo's value, his sway with the university would be significant. Enough to make them reconsider the pansy beds."

Hunter sipped his beer. "Anything else?"

"I think I'm done overusing the word *conserve*."

He grinned.

The alcohol buzz spread to my chest and I was grinning back. Now would be a good time to move this to the dance floor.

"What are you humming about?" Hunter asked, setting down his beer.

"So who's Peter? The love of your life or something?"

Fuuuuuck.

Hunter leaned forward. "I didn't catch that."

Thank Christ. "Nothing. Never mind." I collapsed onto the low stool opposite him. "Maybe you could introduce me to your parents?"

Hunter's eyes flashed. "So soon?"

I rolled my eyes. "I meant, about the gazebo. For an article."

Someone shifted beside me, and Hunter's gaze jumped to my side. "Quinn."

Quinn set down three drinks. "Where'd Liam go?"

"He's chasing after a pen. He had an idea and ran out of ink."

A soft smile touched Quinn's lips. "That's my guy."

Quinn gestured toward the dance floor. "Since no one else seems to be asking," he said with a flickered look my way. "Dance?"

Hunter backed out from the table. "Hell yeah." Quinn hoofed toward the dance floor and Hunter rolled past me, pausing. "You look damn hot tonight, Marc."

I replayed that sentence a thousand times while Hunter spun on the dance floor—and holy shit. He had moves. He grabbed Quinn's hand and twirled him around his chair. Quinn pressed a hand against Hunter's chest, and Hunter whirled around elegantly. He spun and spun and spun. The skill, the strength.

The sexy.

I ordered a rum without the Coke and downed glass after glass, watching him.

Hunter had a life. He had his shit together.

Liam was sitting at the table scribbling into a notebook. Ice rattled in my glass as I stumbled to him. Sloshing liquid over my hand as I sat, I laughed. "Liam. Liam, Liam, Liam."

His head shot up. "You're inebriated."

I finger-gunned him. "You might be right. The last drink hit fast."

Liam pushed over a tall glass. "It's water, I haven't touched it."

"You're giving it to me?"

"You need it."

"But I've been suuuuuch a dick to you."

Liam blinked back an unidentifiable emotion. Hurt? Pride?

Whatever it was, it wasn't indifference.

I drank the offered water, then choked on it when a linebacker in a rainbow T-shirt took over swinging Hunter around the dance floor.

"What are you muttering about?" Liam said.

I snapped my mouth shut. "Not muttering. Observing. I mean, it's okay to watch Hunter dance—"

"With a potential hook up?"

I growled at him, but a hiccup ruined the effect. "That guy isn't his hook up."

"He's a grown man, he can go home with whoever he wants."

I ground my teeth against the aching truth. "I know."

"Just because you like him and he thinks you're hot, doesn't mean he'd seriously consider taking you home."

"Thanks for the honesty."

"And if he ever did, it wouldn't mean anything."

"Do you always speak your mind?" Another hiccup. I rubbed my belly.

Liam frowned and ducked his head. "I veer toward analytical. I don't understand emotion as well as others. I never mean to hurt anyone."

I twisted the icy glass of water in my hand, "I didn't know that."

"What?"

"Why don't you tell people?"

"That I'm on the spectrum? I'd rather not. I like my life and I have friends now."

"Maybe I wouldn't have been such an ass if I'd known."

"Maybe you shouldn't have been anyway."

I nodded and the room tilted slightly. I was seeing double of Liam's glasses. "Can I tell you something?"

"Yes. Whether or not I'll want to hear it is another matter."

I hitched a thumb toward Hunter. "He looks like Chace Crawford with tattoos."

"Who's Chace Crawford?"

"*The Boys?*" I prompted. Liam shook his head. "*Twelve?*" Another shake. "Nate Archibald in *Gossip Girl?*"

"Nope, sorry."

I shook my head, and the buzz followed. "Never mind. He's hot. The build, the hair, the damn fine eyes."

"This conversation just got awkward."

"It helps to have drunk half the bar."

I dropped my head into my arm. Shutting my eyes might clear up the fog. And the disappointment.

A warm hand landed on my shoulder and I startled upright, hoping it was Hunter. It was Quinn. "You all right?"

Hunter was dancing with—*Red Jeans?* When did he get here? I'd thought that was over.

I shrugged Quinn off. "I'm good. Should be heading home."

I rushed out a goodbye, ignored Quinn's sympathetic wince, and hit the men's room for a quick piss. A better guy would swing past Hunter before leaving. I bolted for the exit.

It was just a kiss. We can forget about it.

Hunter had said it himself.

Fresh air breezed across my over-heated face and limbs. I sucked it deeply into my lungs, and stumbled down the street.

I heard my name in the distance behind me. I groped for the nearest lamppost and scanned the street. Hunter wheeled hard and fast along the pavement, a stern set to his jaw. He stopped with a sharp turn toward me. "Why're you running off?"

I nicked my chin in the direction of the club. "You were having fun."

"Yeah, I was hoping it would get more fun once you came over to dance."

"Red Jeans was all over—"

"A little jealousy is cute, Marc," he said softly, "but don't overdo it. He was with someone else, our dance was platonic, and there's plenty of space between us."

I knocked my head back against the lamppost. "You are way too mature for me."

"Maybe it'll rub off."

A laugh tickled out of me.

Hunter started rolling down the street and I followed by his side.

He side-eyed me. "What I saw of you was nice."

"Nice?"

"Really nice. You and Liam hanging out."

I rolled my eyes, secretly glad he thought so. "Never believed you'd see it, huh?"

"Sure, I did. I'm just surprised how quickly."

His belief in me was unexpected. And touching.

"We're civil," I said gruffly, wishing the road wasn't dancing. "We'll never be BFFs."

Hunter snagged my hand. I stumbled toward him and he firmly cupped my hips, steering me onto his warm lap. I gasped. "What are you doing?

His chest pressed against my back, one arm tightening around my waist, his voice pebbling at my ear. "Feet on mine. I'm giving you a ride."

Muscles in his arms and chest flexed around me as he rolled us down a moonlit, oak-lined street. A hoot trumpeted out of me and I sagged against him, resting my head on his shoulder. Orange leaves rained gently over us.

Hunter stopped outside the ramp to his house under an iron-wrought lantern. Soft light glowed over his face and I shifted on his lap to ensure the best view. His eyes danced and that damn mouth would ruin me if I didn't taste him again.

I touched his cheeks and his eyes briefly fluttered shut. I leaned in, nose tapping his, and stopped, groaning.

"I can't."

"Kiss me?"

I nodded but didn't move back. "I'm too drunk." I closed my eyes and breathed him in. "I need to remember it."

Hunter swallowed, and his hand cradled my jaw, thumb sweeping across my cheek. No one had ever looked at me like that. My stomach jumped toward my throat.

Did Hunter feel the same thing? Except—

I scrambled off Hunter. "Is it unrequited? Or are you in an open relationship?"

His eyebrows popped to his hairline. "Excuse me?"

"Peter."

"Peter?"

"Liam let it slip, that you love him. Like, crazy love."

Hunter's head arched back as he laughed.

I folded my arms and scowled at him. "So, what is it? How close are you?"

Hunter scrubbed his jaw over another laugh. "I do love Peter."

"But? I mean, you flirt with . . . guys . . ."

He threw me a no-nonsense look. "I flirt with you."

I shifted from foot to foot, and grabbed the support of the rail. "Yeah."

Hunter rolled past me to the house entrance. "There's nothing physical about Peter and I. Christ. That would burn. At most, Peter watches."

I trailed after him into a brightly tiled foyer. "So he's into voyeurism. And you love him."

Hunter shook his head. "I'll be talking to Liam about this."

"No. I'm glad he told me. I'd rather know."

"I'll introduce you."

I shuddered. "No, don't. I'm good."

"I think Peter would make you laugh."

I huffed under my breath. "Funny is so overrated. Anyone can crack a joke."

"Let's see you do that with a splitting headache in the morning." Hunter keyed open a door and held it wide. "Welcome to my humble abode."

I entered, drunk and curious. Spotless hardwood floors and space. Everything clean and tidy. And *green*. How many plants did he own?

He gave me the grand tour. The apartment had been modified for wheelchair ease. Lower counter surfaces and drawers, and space to roll under the sinks in the bathroom and kitchen.

Hunter ushered me to a large wooden workstation that doubled as a table. I took the guest chair and admired the low-hanging baskets of herbs. Basil. Chives. Rosemary.

"This place looks like that witch's cottage we stayed in." Were my words slurring? "You totally were playing house online!"

Hunter said nothing, but there was a secret quality to his shrug I hoped I'd remember to analyze tomorrow.

"Right," he said. "I'm getting some carbs in you."

THIRTY MINUTES LATER, I was inhaling the most delicious pasta of my life. There was conversation, sure, but I couldn't quite keep up with it.

This lemon-parmesan goodness was insane.

Hunter cocked his head, leaning back in his chair. "You know what you need, Marc? Team-building exercises. Your life in someone else's hands. Close your eyes and fall, and feel the relief of someone catching you."

I finished my plate and eyed Hunter's half-eaten one. "How do you fall when you don't deserve to be caught?"

Hunter leaned forward with purpose. "Close your eyes. I'm going to give you a taste."

I obeyed Hunter's commanding voice.

Cupboards opened, water ran, and a knife bluntly tapped a board.

Hunter disappeared and the toilet flushed. The bin behind me opened and shut.

"Ugh, I'm not sure I like this game."

"Trust exercise." The soft scent of Hunter filled my next breath. The heat of him moving close to my side. "Open your mouth."

"What did you pull out of the bin? What came from the toilet?"

Hunter stroked my nape. "I won't feed you anything you wouldn't eat yourself. Open."

I hesitated, squished my eyes shut, and parted my lips.

"Wider. It's bigger than that."

"Remember I'm hammered and want to be awake for the fun stuff."

A soft slap met the back of my head. I laughed and opened my mouth.

"Yeah, like that."

Something round, smooth, and tangy hit my tongue and I sucked it in and chewed. "Cherry tomato."

"Again."

I opened for him. "Apple slice."

"Again."

I barely hesitated to open up for him now. "Oh my God, that tastes amazing."

"Pesto, homemade."

A fork clattered. From his plate? Pasta slid into my mouth and I hummed around the fork, feeling it vibrate. Did Hunter feel it too?

I opened my eyes.

Hunter pinched the end of the fork, a hitched expression on his face. He laughed. "I saw you eyeing my plate. You can have the rest." He dragged his unfinished pasta to me. "See, Marc? You have it in you."

"Your amazing food?"

He gave me a dirty look. "I know you don't have shit for brains."

I understood. I had it in me to trust Hunter. I had it in me to ease my defenses.

At least, I had it in me while drunk.

Before I knew it, I'd found Hunter's bedroom and thrown myself across his bed. Hunter excused himself for the bathroom, and I studied the plants on his windowsill while playing with a black marker I found on the bedside table.

The bed dipped and Hunter transferred himself next to me.

Shirtless, he'd changed into flannel pants. I gaped at the inked landscape of his chest. Colorful hummingbirds mid-flight, perched on branches, glorious wings expanded.

Clickity-click.

I rolled onto my side. Hunter shifted his leg over a body pillow and faced me.

I pressed the capped marker against the bird over his heart. "Why hummingbirds?"

"They're fascinating. When they appear they always bring joy."

"True. My mom and I saw one once, we kept urging each other to take a photo because neither of us wanted to take our eyes off it. It was a good day."

Hunter smiled. "Exactly. They remind us to enjoy the moment." He removed the marker from my grip and brought my fingers to the small, flying beauty. His warm chest flexed under my touch and the pads of my fingers slid over the soft skin at his nipple. It hardened under me and he quickly moved my fingers to another bird at his collarbone. "A hummingbird can travel up to 2000 miles to reach its destination. Talk about endurance."

His blue eyes wondrously took me in. God, I so badly wanted to kiss him.

I inched my head across the pillow and the room see-sawed. "Hummingbirds complement you," I said. "They're unique, they can fly backwards, sideways and hover, they're adaptable and colorful. Like you."

"They remind me to accept change with grace. They remind me that there's magic in the world, and maybe one day—"

I ran my fingers down his bicep and squeezed his elbow. "Gonna finish that, Hunter? Or do you need trust-building exercises, too?"

He gaze connected with mine, and my heart whirred like hummingbird wings. I whispered, "What does it feel like to you when we look at each other like this?"

"Frighteningly hopeful."

I licked my dry lips. "It's late."

"It is."

"I want to stay here. Not do anything, just . . ."

"Yeah, Marc. I want that too. I wanted you in my bed from the second you walked into the bar tonight. Before that, actually."

Oh, hell. I had better remember this in the morning.

CHAPTER NINE

"So, last night . . ."

His rumbling words near my ear woke me up. I froze. I was in Hunter's bed, drowning in soft cotton pillows, sheets wrapped around my naked body.

"Last night?" We ate pasta, I invited myself to stay, we bonded over hummingbirds . . . "Nothing happened last night."

Hunter's scoffed words tickled between my shoulder blades. "Of course something happened last night."

Really? I didn't feel sore. Oh God, I'd had that wonderful dream I was pushing my cock in a tight, warm—Fuck, did I maul Hunter?

"Stop looking petrified."

"My back's to you," I said. "How do you know I look petrified?"

"You're tensing. I can extrapolate."

"Could you extrapolate on why I'm naked in your bed?"

"You insisted on stripping before climbing under the sheets. Something about not wanting to hide anything from me."

Sounded vaguely familiar. Part of my drunken epiphany about

trust right before sleep consumed me. "What do you mean something happened last night?"

"You came to Phoenix."

I twisted, facing a haughtily amused Hunter. Relief shimmered through me and I shoved his chest. "I told you, I go there all the time." Hunter's sleep-wrecked hair was sexy. "Quite surprised to see you there, actually."

Hunter rolled his eyes and shoved me back. I went with the touch, rolling onto my back. Hunter propped himself on his elbow and twisted the black marker between his fingers.

I raised a questioning brow.

"I've been thinking of getting another tattoo." He uncapped the lid.

The pen touched my smooth chest, cold and wet. He drew curved lines. Leaves. The marker drifted over my hard nipple and I bit my lip on a sensual shiver. More leaves, lower, pen dancing over my abdomen, lower, drawing a teasing line where the sheets pooled at the top of my pubic hair. "You have nothing to hide, Marc."

"I couldn't now if I wanted to." The outline of my half-hard dick was obvious.

"No." He drew more leaves along my side and met my eyes. "You have nothing to hide."

Our eyes met, and I swallowed. I desperately wanted to kiss him.

I cupped Hunter's cheek, stubble rough against my palm, fingers pinching the soft lobe of his ear. His chest seemed to stop undulating, like he was holding his breath. So was I.

My cell phone beeped from the mess of clothes. My Saturday alarm. I sagged back from the tension. "Oh, fuck. It's ten?"

I lurched out of bed, glad for the reprieve but hating it in equal measure.

I booked an Uber and shimmied into my jeans, commando, like the night before.

Hunter watched me from his bed. He'd collapsed face down, and his tight blue boxers clung to the gentle mounds of his ass. A hummingbird peeked out the elastic waist at one cheek. The firm muscles of his back and tattooed shoulders were on full display.

He caught me ogling and shifted, bracing himself on an elbow. "Why are you hurrying?"

My whole body goosebumped as I lunged for my T-shirt. "I have a standing grocery date with my uncle."

I hadn't seen or heard from Uncle Ben since I'd phoned Jason. Damn, this would be a fun morning.

"Is that all?" I battled down the ball of butterflies in my stomach.

"Sure."

I halted before yanking down my shirt. Hunter's body art came into focus. A picture of a plant with . . . penises dangling from it?

I swung in his direction. "Not the humor I expected after my Willie Stroker fail."

He tossed a pillow at me and I caught it against a chest of ink penises.

"That's a picture of Peter," he said.

The name had me freezing immediately. "Peter?"

Hunter smirked, and there was something devilishly gleeful about it. "My pepper plant."

I peeled back the pillow and stared at my chest. "You love Peter," I muttered. Hunter's smirk twitched. "Your pepper plant."

Hunter shifted his leg and sat against the headboard. I hoped he didn't notice my shoulders sagging with relief.

Because, like, he could love whoever he wanted to.

Didn't matter to me.

"I've gotta run, but we'll talk about your love of penis plants later."

"For real. Why are you hurrying?"

I turned my socks the right way and slipped them on, hopping about.

"Marc?"

I gave up on the second sock. "I want to kiss you!"

He looked startled. A laugh pebbled out of him and he patted the bed. "Get over here."

I shook my head, backing to the door. "I can't."

"Give me one good reason."

"Here's three. My mouth is parched, my breath reeks, and my brain is trying to drumroll its way out of my head."

I ducked out of the room before he did any more luring.

Hunter laughed after me. "Don't be long."

I jammed into my shoes and raced out the door. "Another reason I'm hurrying."

I RACED into Uncle Ben's house, stomach balling in preparation for a confrontation. He wasn't in. I grabbed the wad of cash atop the grocery list and took a head-pounding walk to the supermarket.

If only he'd left some indication of his mood. A note or a text telling me that we'd talk about this.

God, he'd done so much for me. Given up so much.

My eyes stung as I stared at a row of frozen pizzas.

"I feel you. Pineapple on pizza is a travesty." I glanced up at Tyler clutching a basket, smiling sweetly.

I blinked rapidly. "Yeah, and they're all out of Supreme."

"Just so happens I took the last one." He pointed to his basket. "I'd ask if you want to share, but I'm pretty sure of the answer."

I winced. "I'm sorry about coffee the other week."

He waved it off. "I jumped to conclusions. Next time we do coffee, it's on me—as friends."

He still wanted to hang out? He watched my lips carefully. "I'd really like that, Tyler."

It came out more desperately than I intended. Could he tell?

He smiled, and I clutched the cart handle. "Anyway . . ."

He nodded. "See you around."

"Enjoy the Supreme."

The checkout assistant rang me up and I grabbed for Uncle Ben's cash, and hesitated.

"That'll be $98.25, sir," he repeated.

I drew out my credit card. I had some savings from summer jobs. Not much, but enough for buying clothes and games. This, though, felt like my best investment.

I stared at my dozen bags of shopping, and laughed so hard tears dampened my eyelashes.

"Marc," Hunter answered cheerily when I called.

"Would you, ah, do me a favor? Usually Uncle Ben drives to the store. Not today, and I didn't think things through . . ."

Hunter chuckled, and the sound of keys jangled in the background. "Yeah, sure. We can track down V.A. right after. Where are you?"

"The Giant Eagle parking lot on Murray, contemplating guzzling a gallon of iced coffee."

"An entire gallon?"

"This headache is killing me, and I love coffee. Good for all that nervous twitching."

"Good for that bright, caffeinated aura, you mean. You won't be hard to find."

He hung up and my belly flipped. There was no way I could drink *any* coffee if I wanted to keep it down.

———

HUNTER KEPT the van running while I dropped the grocery bags off and retrieved the Archie tin. Within ten minutes, we were hurtling in and out of traffic. I found an abandoned magazine at the side of the door and read the *Ask Adam* advice column.

"Dear Adam: My brother is a picky ass and doesn't realize it. He's interviewed, accepted, and then evicted five roommates in the last four months. I'm afraid he'll never find the perfect person to live with, and if he can't find that, how will he ever find a life partner? Response: Time to help him overcome his quirk. Get creative, raise the stakes, and dare your brother to last a month with someone?" I snickered. "Does Adam ever give *sage* advice?"

Hunter grinned. "Want another confession?"

I eyed him suspiciously. "Dunno. Your others weren't exactly treats."

"You'll like this one."

I braced for it. "Try me."

"I sent in a letter once."

"No way."

"Yes, way."

"About what?"

"Dear Adam: I'm depressed at being paralyzed from the waist down . . ."

"Oh."

Hunter winked at me. "He gave sage advice that time. Promise. Told me if I missed basketball so much, I should damn well continue to play."

I smiled softly. "Well. Good. Yeah. You certainly ripped up the court."

Finally, Hunter parked and we disembarked. Hunter gestured up the road. "Vaughn Alexander lives at number one-eighteen."

"Why didn't we drive up?" I side-eyed him with a teasing shake of my head. "This better not be some thinly veiled commentary. I've started jogging again, you know."

Hunter laughed. "There's never parking spaces up there. You're jogging?"

"I have abs I'm not ready to say goodbye to yet."

"I enjoyed saying hello to them, too."

The ink of his tattoo pen soaked shivers into me. "This way, you said?"

We headed up the street.

I stared down a row of oaks, touching my chest over Hunter's artwork. "About Peter . . ."

Hunter let out a dreamy sigh. "So hot."

I scowled, eliciting a smirk. "You *name* your plants?"

His gaze skipped to my hand, and he smiled quietly. "Geek Force, here."

"That's for sure."

Hunter pushed on his wheels, arms flexing. "It's from the tongue twister. Peter Piper picked a peck of pickled peppers, how many peppers did Peter Piper pick?"

"You named him Peter to show off how fast you can recite that line?"

Hunter swerved his chair and lightly bumped my leg. I laughed, and he grinned back. "You got me."

"I'm sufficiently impressed. And superiorly glad Peter isn't a boyfriend. Not sure how I feel about fooling around with a guy who's in love, no matter how open the relationship."

Hunter fumbled his next push and his chair jerked. He quickly corrected it. "I've tried a lot of things, but I've only had one boyfriend before, and we were exclusive."

"The guy you skinny dipped with?"

"You remembered."

"You expected me to forget?"

His laugh bounced around us. "Charlie. Or Captain Cheese."

"What?"

"I used to call him that. In my head. To him, on occasion." Hunter's lips twitched up fondly. "He was captain of our basketball club."

"Skip to the part where his cock smells of cheese," I growled.

Hunter rolled his eyes. "His cock smelled great."

"Something really gross better happen with his face and some cheese very soon."

"Nothing like that happened."

"Then where did the cheese come from?"

Hunter snickered. "He was full of it. Always upbeat, always something sappy to say. Cheesy as hell."

I grumbled about it being a misleading nickname as Hunter watched me. "You're grinning super-hard man. Do you dig cheesiness?"

Hunter's expression morphed into something fucking mournful. He batted his eyes, a dreamy smile on his lips. "If you were at a kissing booth, I'd buy all your kisses."

I blinked at him and groaned. "Piss off."

Hunter smoothly kept pace beside me. "Falling for you is easier than breathing."

I muttered to myself. "I never should have asked."

"Just talking to you, my heart's at risk of exploding."

"Seriously, go to hell."

"I could survive a million fiery deaths as long as you're by my side."

I increased my pace and flipped him off. He laughed.

"Have fun with Peter," I called back to him. "He's the only pickle you're getting."

Hunter choked on a laugh, and I was glad I'd stormed ahead so he didn't catch me smothering my own.

Number one-eighteen was a fenced-off cottage with concrete steps leading to the front door. I stopped at the base. "Are you going to kick my ass if I offer to help you up?"

Hunter swiveled his chair around. "There's a rail here, so if I were alone, I'd get myself up. But it's a little tricky. I won't kick your ass."

I gripped the back handles of his chair and pulled him up the five steps. The path flattened and Hunter resumed gliding beside me. "Thanks."

"Does it bother you? People helping?" I paused. "Or using idioms like 'kick your ass' without thinking?"

"Idiom away. I get it. As for people helping . . ."

I winced. "Yeah, you seem independent."

His expression softened. "Thank you. Most people mean well when they help, and I'm okay with it."

"Right."

"I'd rather rely on kind offers of help than compromise on an outing."

But he'd prefer to manage most situations on his own. Got it. "And, like, what about . . ." Could I ask?

Hunter rubbed the back of my thigh, his go-to spot when I stood next to him. His touch felt like a warm tattoo. Still there long after his fingers dropped away. "What, Marc?"

I helped Hunter up the step to the vine-framed porch. "Would you let someone piggyback you places?"

"Maybe. If they're cute and I can nibble kisses on their neck." Hunter swiveled around. "Though they might need to work on their strength."

I gave him a soft smack on the back of his head. Oh fuck, his hair was so soft. "Hey, I'm strong."

Hunter gave me a soft, curved grin. "I guess you'll have to prove it to me sometime."

"YOU'RE good at hacking info about people," I said after we said goodbye to Vaughn Alexander and I helped Hunter down the stairs.

"Uh huh."

The sun stretched warmly through the orange-leaved trees, dappling the sidewalk and us. The scent of cut grass filled the air.

I studied Hunter's profile: strong set jaw, copper-blond lashes, perfect ear shell.

"Like, really good," I said suspiciously.

His arms flexed, a knowing tilt at his lips, a bright spark in his eye. "What's your point, Marc?"

"You had to know he was married to a woman, that Vaughn wouldn't be our V.A."

"Well. I couldn't know for certain."

I watched him carefully, counting every tic. "Is the other V.A. married?"

"No."

"Kids?"

"No."

"Why didn't we start with *that* V.A. then?"

Hunter spoke simply. Matter of fact. "I wanted the day with you to last longer."

Shivers flurried in my belly. I stepped behind him and halted his chair, gripping the handles hard.

Hunter tipped his head back at me with a curious frown. "Marc—"

I kissed him.

My lips trembled over his, and Hunter stiffened under me for one excruciating heartbeat before he sucked in a breath and kissed me back. I squeezed the handles as I held back a whimper. A soft slotting of his lips, his nose tapping my chin, my mouth moved, fast and urgent over his. My tongue stole into his mouth and I was rewarded with the slippery touch of his locking around mine as if to pull me closer.

His callused fingers pressed into my neck as he clutched my head, palms cupping my ears.

He tasted like peppermint, like he'd expected this moment, and that made me kiss him harder.

"Are your brakes on?" I murmured into flustered kisses.

"Yes."

I released the handles and ran my hands over his shoulders, spreading my fingers wide as I pushed down his chest, over his nipples to his abs. He groaned and broke from the kiss, not letting my head go, keeping me close. He caught his breath and drew me into another kiss.

Softer this time, he dragged the surface of his lips over mine.

"I want more," he said. My dick wanted to drill out of my damn jeans. "I want to see you lose yourself when I fuck you."

"Now? Like, in your van?" I asked. Totally for it, even if I was shaking.

He let my head go and tugged my arm, urging me around his chair. He pulled me onto his lap and breathed me in. I squirmed at the drag of air over my neck.

"Not in the van. Not for that. At least, not the first time."

The idea we could fool around more than once made me dizzy. I couldn't forget the expiry date!

He nibbled kisses and I let out a gravely mantra of "fuck" as he rolled us to the van.

Hunter chuckled. "I promise there'll be lots of that later."

"Later?"

His laugh zipped directly to my balls. "We have a gazebo to save."

That. Right. Yes.

Reluctantly, I climbed off him. "How do you feel about stopping for coffee before heading to our ultimate V.A?"

Hunter unlocked the van, lips raw from our kisses. "How about lunch?"

CHAPTER TEN

Except we didn't accomplish lunch. Or coffee.

After twenty minutes of me squirming in the van, Hunter swore under his breath. "Yeah, okay. We've got to do something about that."

He swerved into an abandoned parking lot overlooking a torn-down factory and a forest.

"By 'that' do you mean the erection that won't go away?"

Hunter pulled the brakes. "Uh huh."

"It's just . . . I tried to think of grannies and giving birth out of my ass and all things unsexy, but you are *right there*."

Hunter searched my eyes and snapped open his seatbelt. "Come closer."

I unbuckled and slid nearer, heart punching up my throat. "So this is it? We're officially fooling around?"

"Shove your pants down."

Holy fuck, I got harder. I scrambled to unzip, shoved my pants around my thighs, and squeezed my rigid shaft.

Air stirred around my cock, and Hunter didn't hesitate. His fingers wrapped around me. I dropped my hands to the vinyl at the exquisite sensation of someone holding me.

He gave me a languid stroke, and there was nothing shy about his grip or his look. He deadlocked my eyes and stroked again. I shook, holding myself from bucking into it, wanting each of his fingers against my silky skin, rubbing over the hardness beneath. Sensation riddled my body.

My hands bore into the vinyl. "That feels so good, Hunter."

He wrung his hand and I convulsed into curses. I wouldn't last long.

"Look at me, Marc."

Hunter's eyes were bright blue, his lips wide and dark. I hooked the corner of his mouth with my thumb. I leaned in and licked his bottom lip. "Such a mouth."

Hunter smiled, hot tongue flicking over the pad of my thumb. "Okay, Marc."

He braced his hand against the dashboard under the Archie tin and descended toward my dick. Hot breath fanned over the head, and his warm mouth suctioned around me.

My toes curled in my sneakers, and I made choking gasps as Hunter consumed me wetly and my dick prodded the tight muscles in his throat.

I rubbed up and down his flank while threading his soft hair. So. Damn. Phenomenal.

Yet I couldn't figure out why—I'd had guys deep throat me before. But this felt intense.

Spontaneity, perhaps?

The butterflies in my chest thrashed wildly, and I wanted so badly to let go. To give in to Hunter and *be*.

Hunter's swollen mouth knew every trick that got me off. My fingers made a mess of his hair, his T-shirt was halfway up his back, and my blunt nails were digging moons into his side.

We were in his van, in a forgotten part of the city, and the surroundings made me think of being lost and alone, except I wasn't. I was with Hunter, and I was cursing his name. Pleading for him never to stop. Arching my ass off the seat, desperately chasing friction.

Holy fuck, what would it feel like when he fucked me?

When I fucked him?

My dick pulsed and Hunter's face wrecked with desire as my dick stretched his amazing mouth. "Hunter," I warned. Begged. Something. "Hunter—"

My orgasm punched through me, and I stiffened, riding the waves of ecstasy as Hunter gulped my come.

He pulled off, sucking every drop; I sagged against the seat, catching my breath. I balled a hand into his T-shirt and urged him closer. "Damn." I kissed him through hitching breaths.

He pulled back and cocked his head. "Grannies, and *giving birth out of your ass?*"

"Like omegas? 'Cause that has to hurt."

"I'm surprised you kept your erection." He snapped on his belt and started the car. "I must really do it for you."

I zipped up, burning, and boldly met his eye. "Fuck yeah."

———

The remaining twenty-minute drive, I hummed along to the radio. I'd turned it on to ward off the silence and awkwardness after such a mind-blowing orgasm.

Elton John's "Don't Go Breaking My Heart" blared out of the speakers and thanks to Uncle Ben I knew every lyric.

Apparently so did Hunter, because we lip-synced the entire song.

I turned down the volume, laughing. "Jesus Christ we're dorks."

"You haven't stopped grinning."

"Shut up," I said, and grinned harder.

VICTOR ALBACORE LIVED in Squirrel Hill, in a brick American foursquare with a tiny hedge lining a dozen concrete steps to the porch.

No rail in sight, I helped Hunter up again, noting his slight unease. Maybe twice in one day was too much.

"Thought you said you didn't mind people helping?" I murmured.

His shoulders tensed.

"Am I doing it wrong?"

The grin he gave was pure plastic and it hurt to witness it. "It's fine."

I rang the doorbell, muttering. "Whatever."

Hunter opened his mouth to reply, but the door opening had him slamming his mouth shut. Or maybe it was the familiar dark-haired woman in yoga pants and tank top.

I blinked. "Hannah?"

Her expression mirrored ours: total surprise with some hard *wtf* brow creases.

A notable scowl twitched at her lips when she saw me. The last time she'd seen me, I'd been tossing wine over Hunter.

I ignored a guilty pull at my gut. "What are you doing here?"

She planted her hands on her hips. "Me? What are *you* doing at my uncle's house?"

Hunter scrubbed his jaw and laughed. "May we come in? We'll explain everything."

WE EXPLAINED that we wanted to interview Victor Albacore for an article. He wasn't in.

We sat in a bright room surrounded by antique furniture and porcelain vases, muffins resting on floral plates. It would be warm and cozy if Hannah stopped frowning at me.

"You're really friends?" she asked Hunter again, as if his first answer had been given under duress.

"Yeah." Hunter pried off the top of his lemon muffin while I tried drilling a hole into mine with my gaze.

She glanced my way and I cracked, foot jiggling under the table. "We met anonymously online. He saved my ass from a Kalvaleth demon's poison and has been saving me ever since."

Hannah sank deeper into her cushion-backed chair. "Huh—"

"He's funny, he makes me laugh. He calls me out on my shit."

Hunter gave my thigh a comforting squeeze under the table. I stopped jiggling.

Hannah nodded. "Okay."

"I've tried to figure out what's wrong with him. Something gross or fucked up, but he's never once stuck his finger up his nose or smiled crookedly while holding a sharp knife. The only thing he lacks is common sense." I tapped my chest. "He seems to like me back."

Hunter rubbed my thigh and met Hannah's eye. "It's like this: I don't mind holding his baggage, and so far, he doesn't mind holding mine."

I stared at Hunter's soft smile and . . . felt itchy inside. Kind of pissed off, too, because if he meant that, surely he wouldn't have thrown up that fake grin outside?

Hannah bowed her head. "God, sorry I'm being so rude."

I cleared my throat. *Moving on.* "How well do you know your uncle?"

"Pretty well. Actually, he's my great uncle and he helped raising my mum. I come here every second weekend." She paused. "What do you want to interview him about?"

"We think he used to be in a relationship with Kyle Gable Green in the seventies."

Her chair skated over tile as she stood sharply. "How do you know that?" She flushed and resumed her seat, hard, gaze darting away from us. "I mean, I don't know what you're talking about."

So. Victor Albacore was definitely our V.A., and Hannah was a terrible actress.

Squirrelly excitement had me bouncing my foot again.

"Look," Hannah said tightly, giving in, "all I know is that they had a past and their friendship broke apart."

"It was more than friendship," I said. We'd left the letters in the van, unsure whether it was our place to pass them on to Victor.

Hannah's breath hopped on a sigh. "That's why you crashed the alumni party?"

"Pretty much," I said.

"He's not here until tomorrow. I'm house sitting." She glanced at her phone. "Actually, I have to hurry to my yoga class, so . . ."

I peered down the hall as she ushered us toward the door. "Uh, could I use your bathroom?"

Hannah gestured around the corner. "Two doors on the right."

Hunter engaged Hannah in jovial-sounding conversation while I peeked around. The study held particular interest, especially the framed picture of our gazebo.

My gaze snagged on a second photo of Victor and Hannah. I recognized the man as the one I'd plowed into exiting the gallery at the alumni party.

He and Kyle had been in close proximity.

I rejoined Hunter and Hannah, who both looked at me like they knew I'd been up to no good. "Nice place. Seriously nice."

"Yeah," Hannah agreed, squinting at me. "Super nice, and super affordable."

I ignored her knowing look, grinned, and continued to bull-shit. "So, tell me more . . ."

Back in the van, Hunter wore an amused, disbelieving look. "What did you find out?"

"Was my sleuthing really that obvious?"

He started the engine. "At least you flushed the toilet for appearance's sake."

"Oh, I actually had to go."

He shook his head, smiling. "And that probing chat on rentals?"

"Can't live in my uncle's basement forever."

Hunter turned away from me, pinking slightly.

I cleared my throat. "Could you geek force more info about Victor's rental agency?"

"Sure. What did you find in Victor's house?"

"A picture of the gazebo."

"That's it?"

"What do you mean, 'that's it?' It means something."

"If you say so."

"I do." I squinted at him. "What was up with the fake-fucking-grin on the porch?"

Hunter rubbed his jaw. "It frustrated me that I needed your help."

"That's it?"

"Your help. Again."

"What do you mean, *my* help?"

His chuckle was hollow, exasperated. "It's not the impression I want to make on you."

He flushed, gripping the steering wheel.

Oh. "You think it could change my mind about fooling around with you?"

He kept his eyes on his hands. "I think it could change your mind about staying my friend."

I leaned over, turned his face toward me, and kissed a startled breath out of him. "Good to know I'm not the only idiot here."

I resumed my seat and turned up the radio. Hunter blinked at me for three long seconds, started the car, and drove.

CHAPTER ELEVEN

After a coffee and a sandwich at the Crazy Mocha, Hunter dropped me off. Liam and Quinn needed his van to transport new furniture.

"There's another party tonight," he said as I hopped out the van. "If you don't mind making nice with my friends two evenings in a row?"

I'd walk over burning coal if it meant more time with Hunter.

I spent the afternoon gutting my basement and making it immaculate.

Time ticked with aching slowness, and all studying done, I found myself reading K's letters and archiving Demon-Slayage chats.

Those were starting to addict me.

I dressed for the party in tight jeans and a fresh red T-shirt the same color as Hunter's carnation gift.

I upended my bathroom cupboards searching for pre-lubed condoms, which I snuck into my back pocket. I startled when Uncle Ben did a double take through the cracked door.

"Hey, Marc. Looking for the Lysol . . ."

I swallowed the awkwardness. "Uncle Ben, yeah. It's . . ." I grabbed the spray and stepped out of the bathroom.

Uncle Ben took the Lysol, clearing his throat. "So, you and Hunter are . . ."

"There's a party tonight."

He rocked back on his heels. "He's a nice guy, Marc."

Was that a compliment or warning? "Yeah, I know. We're fooling around. Having fun."

"Nothing serious?"

A trepid laugh rattled out of me. "Nope."

Uncle Ben, punched with weariness, scrubbed his short beard. He'd not really come downstairs for the Lysol. "I never date?"

My voice stuttered. "Uh, what?"

I sighed, leaning against my desk close to the Archie tin. "You don't, though. Go on dates."

"That may be true. Did you have to share that with my best friend?"

I narrowed my eyes. "He's not just your best friend."

Uncle Ben straightened a throw blanket draped over my couch. "Why'd you call him?"

"Research for my gazebo article."

"Cut the crap." His eyes bored into mine.

Heat and guilt flushed through me. "I wanted to know."

"Know what?"

"If you two still had something."

"It's casual, Marc. I never wanted you attached to the idea of Jason and me, because most of the year, there isn't a him and me."

"I could've handled it."

"Are you handling it?"

My stomach heaved with frustration. "Yes. It's fine. Let him fuck around if it doesn't bother you."

"Marc."

"Fine, I'm not handling it, okay? You give and give. You deserve better."

"Than Jason?"

"Than *me* holding you back from him!"

Uncle Ben reeled back and I forced a shrug. "I'll move out by the end of the month."

I clutched the edge of the desk.

"Marc, come upstairs. Have coffee with me."

I blinked against the sting in my eye and kept my chin at my chest. "Was I wrong? About you loving him?"

Floorboards groaned, followed by the roughness of his long sigh. "No."

"Was I wrong about you staying apart because of me?"

Uncle Ben said nothing, and my heart cracked.

I nodded, then swiveled away from him until he quietly left. I ripped up the letter of apology I'd written to him, and started again.

WHEN HUNTER OPENED THE DOOR, I marched right into the kitchen. The front door thumped closed in the distance and Hunter rolled in after me, brow hitched. "You all right?"

"Yes," I snapped, trying to identify the delicious scents coming from his stove. I lifted the lids of two pots to penne and tomato-basil sauce and helped myself to a spoonful.

Hunter yanked me onto his lap. I dropped the spoon and it clattered to the floor. His arm tightened around my waist and his voice was firm but kind. "Are you all right, Marc?"

No. Yes? Fuck, I didn't know.

Frustration mounted and I turned my head to Hunter. His bright blue eyes bore into mine. I kissed him, hard and deep, and Hunter matched every demanding stroke of my tongue.

I growled and pulled back. "I'm in a pissy mood."

"Want to talk about it?"

"No." I scrambled around on his lap and straddled him. "I want to be dicked out. Hard."

Hunter's grip over my hip and nape tightened. "Tell me what happened?"

"I want to forget."

"What about we go for a walk?"

"Don't you want to fuck me?"

"Like you wouldn't believe, but—"

I reached for the button on his jeans. "So how does this work?"

Hunter pursed his lips and sighed. He wheeled us to the kitchen table, opened a small bag attached to his chair, and drew out a condom, bottle of lube, and a cock ring. He had prepared.

I loved his certainty.

He set the supplies aside and kissed me with a long press of his mouth. "I'm going to the bathroom, and I'll be back in ten minutes. Feel free to change your mind."

I shook my head. "I need us to do our worst together."

Hunter bit down on a groan and disappeared to the bathroom. I yanked off my clothes and paced the kitchen in tight boxer briefs, the head of my cock rudely peeking out. Aching to start business.

I needed this.

I shimmied the elastic waist midway down my shaft. If I shut my eyes, I could still feel Hunter's mouth on me.

God his mouth would ruin me. Everything it could do. Everything it would say.

I grabbed the pantry door and lightly banged my head against it. Hunter wanted to know what was going on, but could I tell him?

Shouldn't I shrug it off? Keep things simply sex between us?

The light in the living room stretched into the kitchen. A soft light made amber from the lampshade. Plants hung from baskets, casting oval shadows.

Hunter's place was tidy and spacious. The burgundy feature wall and stacked bookshelves warmed it with a homely touch.

I cupped my balls. Why was I covered in goosebumps? It wasn't like I hadn't been fucked before.

But would it be much different with Hunter? How could I make it good for him?

I'd researched a few things online, but theory and reality . . .

I rubbed myself through the cotton and imagined Hunter's square-tipped, calloused fingers doing the same, dragging over my sensitive skin . . .

A shiver stole over me from scalp to toe. I tugged my balls not to embarrassingly come from the thought alone.

Hunter rolled into the room. The table blocked half of him from view, but his perfectly formed chest and firm, tattooed skin hinted he was naked.

He rounded into the kitchen and paused.

Hunter sat proudly, a hummingbird on either thigh, his flaccid dick resting on smooth balls. His sparse and well-groomed patch of pubic hair made me wonder if I should have waxed my asshole.

Hunter ran a hand through his hair. Was he hiding a tremble?

His nervousness gave me the courage to unstick myself from the door and move to him. "I totally haven't changed my mind," I breathed out.

The corner of his mouth twitched, and he steered me closer by the back of my thighs. His eyes dragged up my obscene under-wear/dick situation to my face. "Made yourself comfortable, I see."

"Right at home."

Hunter's smiled bloomed. "Kiss me."

I smiled into the kiss, trying to stifle a giggle by pressing our mouths firmly together. The giggle shuddered through my chest, and Hunter slid his hands over my abs as if to soak the sound in.

He pulled back. "What's the laugh for?"

Weirdly happy. "Nervous."

He cradled my head. His eyes softened as he took in every feature of my face. His thumbs slid up to my temples, fingers softly scraping up through my hair. I wasn't sure what to do with my hands and braced them on his broad shoulders. "You can sit on me, Marc."

"I won't, like, hurt you—shit that was stupid. I meant squash . . ." I heated, and Hunter smiled with far more patience than I deserved.

"Just like before, only less material between us."

I shuffled onto his lap.

He breathed me in. "Mmm, herby."

"Better than earthy," I growled. "I washed. Thoroughly."

Hunter gripped me around my ribcage. His thumbs rubbed the faded leaves he'd drawn on me yesterday. "How many times do I have to say it? I like your earthiness."

I rocked my dick against his sternum. "Maybe third time is a charm?"

He smashed his face against my armpit and breathed deeply. "I love your earthiness."

He peeked at me. I stared down at him, quiet confidence expanding in the intimate space between us.

I sank back onto his firm, warm thighs. "I have questions."

Hunter tipped my chin down and kissed me. "Ask."

"I thought, maybe . . . I was expecting your legs to be a little, um, atrophied?"

"It can happen. I use electrical stimulation to increase muscle mass."

I squeezed his shoulders. Hunter's eyes blissfully rolled back. "God, I need the gym."

Hunter laughed, light and carefree. His next kiss stole my grin. Deep, slow, and soft, as if we had enough time to infinitely explore each other's mouths. My cock pulsed in synchrony, a slow steady beat.

I gaped at the engorged head and below at Hunter's lap.

"Don't take it personally," Hunter said. "Without a helping hand, he doesn't get up for anyone."

I clasped my hands on his face. "Tell me what you like. So maybe next time we can do this on instinct?"

Hunter sucked in a breath and wheeled us to the table. He uncapped the lube and squirted some onto my palm. Taking me with him, he wrapped my hand around his length and together we stroked. Blood slowly plumped his shaft. "Sometimes, it doesn't last long. The cock ring helps. I have a hollow strap-on, too." He smirked at me. "I really love to top."

"Why?"

"Getting you off makes me feel good." Hot breath curled against my ear. "I'm strong. I'm good at it."

I stroked him faster, angling the head of my cock to bump against the hardening tip of his. "Fuck, Hunter, that's hot. Do you ever switch?"

Hunter smothered more lube over his hand and sent me to the stars with a slick, firm stroke. "I have, once upon a time. With Charlie."

I narrowed my eyes and muttered about the stupidity of cheese. Hunter's expert grip on my dick yanked my focus away from wordage.

His other hand, still wet with lube, slid under the waistband and lightly skimmed over my ass cheek.

I sagged into a frenzied kiss as his fingers drifted to my crack.

"Do you switch?" Hunter asked.

"Actually, I . . . never mind."

I kissed him, and Hunter returned it briefly before pulling back, chuckling. "Hey, we both get to be vulnerable here." He stroked my hair back.

I haven't topped. But . . . "I want to, okay?" I shivered and dropped my gaze. "Not tonight."

Hunter kissed my neck. "Okay."

He nestled a lubed finger down my crack, flat against my hole, and kissed me hard, every slick second of it a blazing turn-on. I pumped his dick, keeping him hard, wriggling my ass to firmly ease his fingers inside me. The chair wheels squeaked against the tile like a debauched promise of what was to come.

"I need my boxers off." But I continued kissing Hunter like he was my only source of oxygen, and Hunter didn't seem hurried to assist. His finger teased the million nerve endings at my ass and his other hand held a massaging grip on my waist.

"Tell me about your fantasies, Marc."

I let go of his cock and braced my palms over his chest at his nipples. "Sexy stuff. The usual."

"Have I been in any of them?"

"In one or two." *All*.

"Hmmm. Am I naked? Am I fucking you?"

"Sometimes. Other times—"

"Other times?"

"We're laughing over a pasta dish you made. Or curled up in big pillows playing Demon-Slayage side by side. Or last night, it was us dancing at Phoenix."

Hunter's grip on my waist slackened. "You fantasize about me romantically?"

A panicked flurry of nerves jerked my gut. "And we always have crazy, wild, primal sex. Like we're about to do now. Right?"

Hunter shook off whatever he'd been thinking. "Right. Crazy. Wild. Primal." He steered me off his lap. "Ditch the boxers."

I stripped, and Hunter placed the lubed cock ring around his shaft and behind his balls.

Ticklish awareness that we were one step closer to *us* happening had me flushing.

Hunter thumped the kitchen table. "Sit up here."

I awkwardly followed his instructions. He parted my legs and rolled between them. His thumbs traveled up my inner thighs. He sat at the perfect level to suck me, and my cock jumped at the memory of us in his van.

I leaned back on the table and reveled in the sensation of Hunter nibbling kisses toward my balls. I loved the easy, practiced way he moved.

I shoved back my disappointment in realizing his skill must indicate he hooks up often. Maybe this wasn't anything special.

The feat was made easier when he started suckling one of my balls.

I melted into a string of curse words and practically died when he spoke at my hole, moist breath vibrating close. "Sling your legs over my shoulders."

I did as he said, resting my thighs at his shoulders. The balls of my feet bore into his back. His hands squeezed my ass and his hot tongue pushed past my ring. I slapped the tabletop. Hunter's tight grip had me frantically thumping the surface.

When he stopped, I was panting, cock so hard it touched my stomach. Hunter's lips were raw, and the only thing I could do was flip him off. "You did that on purpose."

"Teased you to the brink twice?"

I dropped my head back, still catching my breath, and stared at the plants hanging from the ceiling. To my right was a pepper plant. That damn pepper plant. Peter was watching us after all.

Hunter dolloped lube on his finger and breached me, one long thick finger sliding all the way in.

Fuck, we had to do this again. Again, and again, and again.

"Let's fast forward," I pulled my legs off his shoulders and sat upright. Hunter captured the end of my cock in his mouth and I shoved him off with a growl. "I will come on your face."

"As long as you promise to lick it off me."

I grabbed the condom and tore it open. "I need your cock now."

Hunter rolled back for me to stand and before he engaged the brakes, condom pinched between my fingers, I palmed his chair and shoved him across the kitchen to the pantry door.

Hunter's eyebrows shot up as I gave the chair a testing shove.

It struck the door with a nice hollow echo. Hunter's eyes turned molten as he realized what I intended. I expertly pushed the condom over him and straddled his lap.

I positioned him at my entrance, a blunt promising pressure, and paused.

Hunter's dark eyes met mine with lust. His heart pounded under my palm.

"I want this to be good for you too, Hunter."

"Start at my shoulders, go to town on my nipples. When you've come, pull off me, ditch the condom, and suck my neck." He drew a line down his throat and tapped the crook of his neck.

I lightly traced the path he'd drawn and he shivered under me. "Yeah," he said huskily. "There."

I did it again and he captured my mouth into a moaning kiss.

I slowly sank onto him, gasping against his lips. His dick was bigger than I was used to and the stretch burned.

"You okay?" he asked, cradling my face.

My ass pulsed around him, getting used to the intrusion. "Not sure I'm allowed to complain about pain when pain is a privilege."

His fingertips tightened in my hair. "You're allowed to feel what you feel, Marc. You have nothing to hide from me, remember?"

The intensely vulnerable moment made me shiver from head to foot as I held his big blue eyes.

I slowly swiveled my hips, cock tapping against his abs. My tongue clucked as I whispered, "What are your fantasies?"

His nose touched mine and he gripped my cock with a perfect stroke. "I want to see you fall apart in my arms."

"And?"

"I want you to tell me what happened tonight."

I sucked in a breath. "Anything else?"

"Yes."

"Tell me?"

He never avoided my eyes. "I want you in my bed again in the morning."

I shut my eyes on a sting of emotion and concentrated on Hunter's thick length buried in me. My knees bored into the chair, my toes curled, and I lightly scratched his shoulders as I rocked up and down, slowly at first, then gaining length and speed.

I selfishly worked to find the best angle. Hunter braced his chair and his biceps flexed as he jerked himself up, meeting my downward thrust. Holy hell, I was seeing stars.

Hunter's upper body strength . . . My prostate hadn't been this wonderfully abused *ever.*

I dug into his arms and held on, cursing "more" and "fuck-yes" as the chair banged wantonly against the door. Hunter grunted, and I clumsily kissed more sexy sounds out of him.

My fingers trailed over hummingbirds as I rubbed at his nipples.

Hunter pounded into me harder, and I was close. God, so close. I squeezed his hard nubs, licked my fingers, and alternated light touches with hard ones until he was muttering unabashedly dirty words in time to his aggressive thrusts.

I wrung his nipples, clinging on as I let go. My head dropped back as I shot against his chest, four, five, six times. Absolutely wrecked, I wanted to collapse and catch my breath in his tight embrace but not before . . .

I rose off him, tossed the condom, and kissed him, hungry for his tongue against mine. I slid my fingers through my come and over the sensitive length of his neck. Hunter shivered, moaned, and writhed under me.

His breath hitched as he rode a wave of ecstasy, and I wanted it to be the best wave he'd ever ridden. I nibbled his jaw and breathily whispered how fucking hot he was as I dragged my lips down his neck, tasting my come.

When my lips found that soft joint between his neck and his shoulder, I bit down on him and sucked.

His hands flew to his nipples and I slid my fingers between his and rubbed with him.

"…totally destroying me," he groaned and his muscles tightened.

I kissed his throat through the shudders and squeezed our fingers together.

He pulled me fervently into a kiss and massaged my nape. All confidence, no shyness.

Not on his side, anyway.

He drew back and angled my forehead to his. A ticklish flush spread over my body. I busied myself carefully removing Hunter's cock ring.

He took it from me and knotted our fingers together. "How are you feeling?"

"I've never been fucked like that before." I looked at him in wonder. "How long before we can do it again?"

Hunter laughed into a kiss and slapped my ass. Intimate, curiously vulnerable, and wildly fun.

The shrill ring of Hunter's phone interrupted the moment.

He fished the phone from the same compartment as the lube and cock ring.

"Liam," he answered, gaze hitting mine warningly as I attempted to slide off him.

I resettled on his legs, and he absently rubbed my thigh. "We got delayed." He raised an eyebrow at me. "We could be there in thirty minutes?"

Oh. The party.

Awkward socializing with Hunter's friends. The constant reminder I wasn't good enough for Hunter. My insides sank, but I yanked out a grin and nodded.

"See you soon," Hunter said, and hung up. He slid the phone away and palmed my thighs. "Doing it again will have to wait."

"S'good. I need practice in patience."

I wrangled my boxers on. My chest was sticky. Hunter started rolling and angled his head for me to follow. "Come."

Hunter wrung hot water out of a washcloth and passed it to me. I cleaned myself, watching Hunter in the mirror meticulously doing the same. The edge of his washcloth lingered at the red spot where I'd sucked his neck.

I wasn't sure I was meant to see his secret smile, but I did, and it triggered one of my own.

THE PARTY with Liam and Quinn.

Not the most fun. Turned out a couple of Hunter's past crushes were at the frat house, and had decided tonight, of all nights, to return Hunter's past attentions.

I spent most of the evening finding excuses to escape the flirtations to the balcony.

I zipped up my jacket and leaned against the rail overlooking a grassy park. Movement stirred behind me and I turned. Liam seemed equally eager to flee.

"I'm not ready to be friends with you yet," he said matter-of-factly.

"Right. I get it."

"But."

My body jerked straighter at that qualification. But?

"Thank you for editing and submitting my article about dating for the differently abled last year. You didn't have to, and it meant a lot to me you did."

He'd never have submitted it in on time if I hadn't done it. He'd chosen helping his friends over landing a feature article that meant the world to him. It wasn't enough to atone, but it'd helped.

He frowned toward the clear night sky. "Why did you do it?"

The ghost of pain from Jack's punches had me shivering. "I realized I'd been wrong." My hands tightened on the rail. Here was my opportunity to apologize, properly, without the influence of alcohol. "Liam, how I behaved—"

The balcony doors swung out and Quinn stepped outside, carrying Hunter bridal style. Hunter's arms were looped around Quinn's shoulders. I bristled. Sure, the door might not be wide enough for his chair, but I had a phone. Hunter could've called me to get him.

Quinn gently deposited Hunter onto a bench before promptly slipping his arms around Liam and kissing his throat.

Hunter spared me a dirty look. "I can't believe you left me in there to fend for myself."

My mouth dropped open. "You were soaking up those guys' attention."

"For the first five minutes, but then I looked around for you to run away with me, and you'd run away without me."

"I'm feeling a cue for us to leave," Quinn said. He playfully dragged Liam toward the door. "Call me when you want to come back in."

Someone growled.

Apparently, it was me. "I'm gonna need you not to do that. Thanks."

Quinn glanced to Hunter and pulled Liam inside, nodding.

Hunter raised a humored brow. "You've gone all pissy."

"Wanna fuck it out of me?"

Hunter cast me a chastising look.

"What? I mean it." I drew out the condoms. "I'll ride you right there. I don't care who watches."

"Marc . . ."

"It'll be spontaneous. Fun."

"Don't think I wouldn't do it," Hunter growled. "Hell, I don't give a shit who watches."

I prowled toward him. "Come on then, let's do it."

"Talk to me. Tell me something real."

"Something real: this, right here, you fucking me on the balcony. Let's call it a fantasy."

Hunter pulled me onto his lap. My back against his chest, his hot breath puddled under my ear. "What happened earlier today?"

"Just stuff. Nothing important."

Hunter undid my jeans and reached a cool hand into my boxer briefs. He stroked my half-hard cock.

Fuck, Hunter meant it. I groaned and dropped my head back on his wide shoulder.

He kissed my throat and whispered. "What happened?"

My eyes stung, and my chest thumped hard with butterflies and wretched sadness.

The harder I tried to blink it down, the more it fought to the surface. A stupid tear leaked out of my eye, and Hunter kissed it.

"Come on, love, talk to me."

I didn't know what to think of that endearment. Didn't know how to respond. But my chest hopped as words poured out of my mouth. The call with Jason, ruining things with the love of Uncle Ben's life, Uncle Ben's near confession . . . .

My erection wilted, and Hunter slid his arms around my waist and held me tight.

"When I first moved in, Jason came to visit. I was, like, sixteen and a real piece of work. I knew why Dad thought I was a disappointment. I basically told the world to fuck off. Everything annoyed me. Including Jason. He's a ballet dancer and . . . has certain mannerisms. I didn't like how in-your-face gay he was and I let him know it. Not in words, in attitude. In making it uncomfortable. It worked. I'm to blame for their broken romance."

A silent sob wracked my torso and Hunter braced me through it.

"I'm a bad person, Hunter."

Hunter murmured soft comforting sounds, but I was too lost in the stinging ache to hear his words.

"Come on, Marc. Let me drive you home."

I twisted, facing him and his concern. "No, not there."

He thumbed away a stray tear. "Because of how things are with your uncle?"

"Yeah. And . . ."

"And?"

I wanted to wake up in Hunter's bed again. "Never mind."

Together we moved him securely onto my back. He was heavy, but nothing I couldn't manage. I stretched my neck. "Start nibbling."

Hunter laughed, and then started nibbling.

CHAPTER TWELVE

Eight hours later, Hunter transferred himself out of bed for his morning routine. I stretched over his warm vacant space and called out for him to hurry back.

He did, with supplies.

Hunter moved himself behind me and with superior upper-body strength and a strap on, fucked me until I came all over his sheets. I rolled in the puddle and playfully tackled Hunter to the mattress, stroking his neck and nipples until his eyes rolled back and he sneezed.

"There's a link between the nose and genitals," Hunter explained on our way to meet Victor. "Sneezes are like a release of the mounting itchiness inside my chest. My version of an orgasm, I suppose. It feels nice." He eyed me. "That weird?"

"How much of a shit am I if it makes me laugh?"

"An honest one?"

I laughed. "Dude, I'm just glad you get off."

Outside Victor Albacore's house, at the base of his hedged steps, I caught Hunter looking at me. I chuckled, grabbed the handles of his chair, and pulled him up.

In my mind, Victor was an aged man with sad, wise eyes, and

brokenness that clung to him. In reality, he was a fit older gentleman with an enviable crop of hair, and robust, full-of-life vocal cords. His brown eyes crinkled at the edges, and the only thing heavy about him was the way he leaned on his cane when he walked.

"Lost my left foot to a mine in Vietnam," he said by way of explanation, tapping his cane against his metal leg.

We sat at the doily-covered table with steaming lemon tea. Hannah wasn't around, but Victor promised she'd told him what we wanted.

I had the overwhelming urge to give him the Archie tin and tell him to read everything and realize how much Kyle loved him.

But a little tug in my gut said it wasn't mine to give.

"You're here about my relationship with Kyle Gable Green."

We nodded.

I wondered if he could tell there was more between Hunter and me than how we'd introduced ourselves—as a writer and a photographer for the *Scribe*. Hunter had rolled into the close space next to me, and every time he laughed or spoke, I couldn't help but glance at him.

"What happened?" I asked. "From your perspective."

Victor took a long drink of tea. "You want to use my story in an article?"

"Our goal is to save the Lover's Loop gazebo. The more stories we have . . ."

"Have you spoken to Kyle?"

Hunter answered. "Not until next week."

Victor gripped the tiger head of his cane. "I'll have to ask you not to write about our story unless Kyle gives you permission."

"Off the record then?"

His story matched Kyle's down to the horrible way they parted. The jovial tone drained from Victor's voice, and he slumped with the weariness and heartache I had first expected.

I swallowed. "He never contacted you again? You went off to

war and that was it?"

Victor sighed. "No. He came to my house the minute I returned and begged to get back together."

I remembered the aching, regretful sorrow and love of Kyle's letters. Dread sank through my stomach to my toes. "You didn't forgive him?"

My voice sounded hollow. I couldn't meet Hunter's eye.

Victor answered, "I was in a lot of pain, I was angry. I'd lost half my leg."

Desperation hiccupped through me. "He never tried again?

Victor inclined his head and stole my hope for a happy resolution. "He tried once more."

"And?"

"I was broken, boys. He wasn't. And he was important, he didn't need . . ." Victor shut his eyes. "He kissed me, and I told him I couldn't forgive him. That I didn't love him anymore."

I pictured Kyle, desperate on the doorstep, hands trembling as he pleaded for another chance. And Victor barely holding his gaze as he told him to leave and never come back.

I felt the ache of their rift as I imagined the final steps Kyle took away from Victor, head bowed in grief.

Victor continued talking, but I barely concentrated.

When he offered more tea, I declined, lurching to my feet. Every breath felt suffocating and thick in my throat.

Hunter eyed me worriedly and wrapped up for us with kind goodbyes.

In silence, I helped Hunter down the garden steps as Victor watched us from his porch.

Hunter waved before he rolled to the van—and past it.

With heavy steps, I followed him to a local graveyard. Pretty. And morbid; fitting to my mood.

He stopped at a pond filled with giant fish, watching me through the reflection on the surface of the water.

"It was so disappointing," I murmured to his unasked

question.

"Ah."

"I knew they didn't end up together, so I should've expected disappointment, but . . . I thought it was because Kyle never tried." In an alternate universe, they would have lived happily ever after.

What fairytale world did I think I lived in?

I kicked a pebble into the water and it rippled away our reflections. "Aren't you bummed?"

Hunter remained quiet, focused on rows of veteran's gravestones. "I understood Victor."

My knotted gut sank. He took Victor's side? The letters meant nothing? My voice cracked. "You understood?"

"Yes."

Hunter's answer felt like a betrayal. Like confirmation no matter how much I . . .

"Right."

I shuffled away. It was for the best. I didn't want to dig up more emotions than necessary. What was the point, if we fundamentally disagreed?

"Marc?" Hunter called after me.

"I, um, need a walk," I said with a Herculean effort to mask my pain. "I don't live far. I can get myself home."

"Wait—"

Curious frustration in Hunter's tone had me stalling. I glanced at him over my shoulder. "How could you agree with him?"

He stopped rolling after me, hands braced on his wheels. "I just . . . I do, okay?"

I nodded and turned away, nodding some more. "Yep, okay," I said, but I wasn't.

I didn't message him for the rest of the day, and he didn't either.

Our disagreement continued into Tuesday, making that week the crappiest since visiting Jack in prison.

Sunday and Monday, I'd itched to play Demon-Slayage and had compromised by reading chat archives instead. Not because I didn't *want* to talk to Hunter—I did, so fucking much—but realizing that things would never last between us depressed me. I wondered if I should cut my losses.

Uncle Ben muttered about respecting my space and being there when I was ready. Oh, and Jason was flying in this weekend.

Five o'clock sharp, I sat in a creaky wooden chair across the desk from Mr. Wyatt, the senior adviser overseeing the redevelopment of Lover's Loop.

I'd entered on the aggressive, and he flashed his bleached teeth in an impatient smile.

A rap came, and Hunter rolled into the room.

I stopped arguing and stood, rushing out his name in surprise. I mean sure, Hunter said he'd come, but I thought after Sunday he wouldn't.

He wore a nerdy *Byte Me* T-shirt under an open leather jacket, brown jeans, and forest green Pumas. Clean and neat, except for his messy hair. Had he been just as miserable as me?

His eyes shot politely from Mr. Wyatt to me and held, his chest rising on a sharper intake of air.

My heart whickered in my chest.

"Can I join you?" Hunter asked.

I nodded stupidly. *Yes, join us. Please.*

Fuck, I missed you.

He searched my face and I searched his. Uncertainty and something thick and desperate stretched taut between us. I resumed my seat, gripping the base.

Fuck cutting my losses. I was too selfish for that. I wanted to see Hunter again. Surely we could make this fooling around thing last longer.

He swiveled beside me. Maybe?

He turned his attention to Mr. Wyatt and handed over a folder from his chair.

"What's this?" Mr. Wyatt slipped on a pair of spectacles and perused the contents.

"From a simple search online," Hunter said, "there are over a thousand pictures taken of Lover's Loop gazebo by past alumni and the public that imply altruistic feelings about the landmark. Over three hundred scratched initials and locks mark it. It has been used as a set in two local films and one international one. The gazebo has an incredible sentimental value and it should be conserved."

Mr. Wyatt shut the folder. "As I was about to tell Marc before you joined us, the plans to take it down have been in place for months, and the university will most definitely move forward with them."

I cursed. "We'll hold a protest. Rally students, find support."

"It won't change anything."

"It's a way of creating awareness, of being heard."

"Your enthusiasm is admirable, boys, but—"

"What if we ask Kyle Gable Green to step in? His family founded this university, surely he could stop these plans."

"I daresay he could. But that won't happen."

I stood, smiling tightly. "We'll see about that."

Hunter and I moved toward the exit, and Mr. Wyatt called after us. "It won't happen, because Mr. Gable Green was the one who asked for the gazebo to be taken down."

***

"What?" I said, blindly following Hunter across campus. "Like, *what?*"

I still hadn't processed Mr. Wyatt's parting bomb. "How could he?"

I started panting before I realized we were heading up a

familiar zigzag path. My step stuttered and Hunter moved ahead with controlled pushes.

Awareness prickled over me as we moved past the Lover's Loop sign to the evening-haloed gazebo.

The floor was still broken where Hunter had fallen through it. We stopped at the edge of the ramp, staring in. "Why are we here?" I asked softly.

My palms sweated and I clasped my crossed arms under my armpits.

Hunter dropped his gaze and jerked his camera bag to his lap. "It's golden hour."

Rich lighting glazed the classic framework. It was pretty, sure. But was that the reason he'd led me here?

I hoped not.

He rounded the gazebo and roughed it over the grass to take pictures from multiple angles. He stopped at the arched window, crimson roses flanking him, and set his camera on the sill.

"Got the perfect shot yet?"

"A few." He patted the gazebo. "Thing's a real beauty."

His fingers drifted to the side of the arch and rubbed. "Your parents' names?"

"I'm imagining them, twenty-six years ago, maybe kissing on this windowsill before inscribing their names. Dan hearts Mary."

Hunter smiled softly, picked up his camera, and took a shot of it.

"What are they like, your parents?"

"They're a team. They're each other's biggest cheerleader."

"Do you see them often?"

"They visit here a few times a year, and I drive home for major holidays. We call a couple of times a week. Tonight, actually."

I edged inside the gazebo and perched on the sill. Dan and Mary's names glowed. "Were you like the Brady Bunch family?"

"We had our share of fights, but ultimately, yeah."

I laughed. "Sounds nice."

"They'd like you."

"Maybe we should put that theory to the test?" I said, gnawing my bottom lip. "I mean, I want to interview them for the *Scribe* . . ."

Hunter lifted those intelligent blue eyes to me. "Come over at eight-thirty. We'll Skype."

* * *

WE PARTED ways at the *Scribe* office, and five minutes after I'd gotten home, I called an Uber and headed to Hunter's.

I pounded on his door.

Startled, he opened it. "I said eight-thirty. It's six-thirty."

"I'm hungry. Are you hungry? The cute little Italian place up the road makes their own pasta. We could eat and be merry."

Be merry? What the fuck?

"Are you asking me out to dinner? Like a date?" Hunter seemed confused—wary?—and my chest did a panicky leap to my Adam's apple. "There'd be nothing *boyfriendy* about it. More like, two people who need to consume food for survival, doing it together."

"Dinner. For survival?"

I slipped my hands into my back pockets, reaching for calm. "Uh huh."

"Wow." Was that a smile twitching his lips? "What a proposition."

I lifted a brow. "I suppose afterward we could do other things needed for survival."

Hunter snickered, rubbing his nape.

I rocked back on my heels. "It's cool if you're not into the idea. A beautiful man like you probably has a bunch of better offers for dates. I mean dinner."

Hunter's smile softened, and a glimmer of vulnerability illuminated his eyes. He grabbed his leather jacket and keys and pushed past me. I shut the door behind him.

"That's the second time you've called me beautiful."

I halted a step on the ramp, cleared my throat, and caught up to him. "You are, Hunter."

Hunter smiled and we headed for the restaurant side by side.

"Later," he murmured, "after the call with my folks, ask me again about my thoughts on . . . survival."

MARY HUNTER FILLED Hunter's laptop screen with soft-looking sandy curls and a sweet smile. She had Hunter's blue eyes and charming live-in-the-moment confidence.

All the nerves I felt over preparing to meet her melted instantaneously. When she laughed to someone off screen with a vibrant, playful "piss off"—I was in love.

". . . and you're Travis's . . .?" Mary let the sentence hang. I stiffened, and Hunter shook his head, laughing lightly.

"We work at the campus paper together."

Hunter's cheeks flushed pink. Suppose it was awkward to explain we were more like friends with foolery.

Mary spoke like she was teasing, a cheeky twinkle in her eye. "Are you the guy my son has been hanging out with online all summer?"

I snorted. "Are you relieved I'm not a pervy catfisher?"

Hunter groaned.

I clasped Hunter's shoulder, laughing against his bicep. "Your mom wasn't the only one who worried. Uncle Ben, too. Truth? I'm glad you turned out to be you."

Hunter's lips hopped as he gazed back at me. "I'm glad too, Marc."

A tiny smudge of tomato sauce reddened the curve of his mouth, which totally explained why I was staring at his lips.

I startled as a male voice jumped from the laptop. A bearded man wrapped his arms around Mary's shoulders and kissed her cheek. Hunter's dad. They shared the same broad chest and straight nose. "How's it going, son?"

His eyes shifted between us, curious.

Hunter rubbed a palm over a deep smile. "Pretty good. This is Marc."

Dan's eyes glittered. "So good to put a face to the name."

How much had he talked about me? I grinned, flushing. "*Anyway.* There's a purpose for this call."

"I know," said Mary.

"We're interviewing you and Dan about how you etched your names into Lover's Loop gazebo."

"We can do that, too," Dan said, and leaped into the story of how they met. "It was fate. Destiny. We both loved tuna sandwiches."

Mary snickered. "The Grind made the best sandwiches and we finished the same math class before lunch on Tuesdays and Thursdays, so we kept recognizing each other in line. Then one day . . ." Mary shook her head and sighed dramatically.

Dan took over. "There was only one tuna sandwich left."

"And you bought it and gave it to Mary?" I asked.

Dan smirked at his wife and kissed her. "The other way around."

Mary laughed. "Then he got a knife and cut it in half and we shared it."

"Best thing I ever did," Dan said. "We talked all afternoon, and—"

"You lived happily ever after," I murmured.

Mary shook her head. "Not quite. We left, afraid to ask the other out. Unfortunately it was the end of semester, and we had different schedules after the summer."

"What? Stupid," I said, laughing.

Mary smiled. "You know it's true love when you find a person who accepts you, stupid mistakes and all."

"The thing about making mistakes though," Dan said, "is that they have the potential to be lessons, if you learn from them."

"How did you learn from your stupid mistake?"

"The next time I found her," Dan said soberly. "I didn't let her escape."

That attitude was why Hunter's parents had made it. "How did you find her?"

"That was the tricky bit."

I grabbed the arm of Hunter's chair, intrigued, fingers skimming a hummingbird at his forearm. "I want details."

Mary and Dan laughed, and whispered in one another's ear.

"You can't leave me on a cliff like this." I grabbed Hunter's hand. "Tell them, Hunter."

Hunter squeezed his fingers around mine, while Dan faced the camera and asked, "What would you have done in our situation?"

Hunter shook his head, thumb rubbing the back of mine. "Seriously, every time?" He looked at me. "They always do this."

Mary nodded earnestly. "It gives us insight into your character."

I grimaced. "Maybe we shouldn't. You seem to like me so far."

Dan laughed, and Hunter gave me a reassuring squeeze.

"I don't know, buy all the sandwiches and tell the shop assistant to send anyone looking for a tuna sandwich to stop by my table?"

Mary laughed. "Close enough. Dan landed a job at the café hoping to serve me as a customer."

"I started working on Monday morning, and on Monday midday, a new co-worker stepped in to help out with the lunch rush." Dan paused. "Turned out it was Mary."

"We both had the same plan."

"And laughed so hard. We've been together since."

"Awesome," I said. "And the gazebo?"

"Third date. Picnic with tuna sandwiches," Dan said.

Mary nodded. "I cut our names into it with his army knife."

"The third date?"

She shrugged. "When you know, you know."

Huh.

Hunter might be perfect for me, but he deserved better.

Horrible heaviness churned in my gut. I doubled my grip on Hunter's hand until his parents said goodbye.

"Look after our boy," Mary said.

"He doesn't need looking after," I said bluntly, then paused. "But if he did, I would."

Dan's beaming face was the last I saw before the call cut out.

I jumped to my feet and moved to pour a drink even though I wasn't thirsty. "Like, nice parents." I spilled juice down my chin. Fuck. I swiped it off.

Hunter watched me quietly.

"You know what we should do?" I continued. "Call Kyle and make the next possible appointment with him."

"Hmm. In the morning."

I gulped more juice. "Yeah, probably too late. Hey, did you ever find out who Victor's rental agency is? Maybe you can help me scout studio apartments online. You know, something with good access for you to visit." I set my glass down, finally realizing I never handed Hunter his. I slid it over the table. "Or Demon Slayage? I could go home and we can play."

Hunter sipped his juice, blue eyes amused. "I have another laptop. We can play side by side. In bed, if you like?"

WE WERE shoulder to shoulder in bed, pillows stuffed behind us. Reading lamps glowed softly over our laptops.

Hunter had changed into flannel pajama pants, torso bare except for toned skin and hummingbirds. I'd stripped to my boxers and Cheetos-stained tank top. With Hunter around, I didn't need to drown in their cheesy goodness as often anymore.

Sure, he bullshitted his confidence from time to time, but his core was stronger than anyone's I'd met.

DaMage: We need to talk.

Me: About the vampire mages?

DaMage: How are we going to address this?

Me: Chant, and throw holy water at their feet.

DaMage: Not the game.

Me: Figured. Look, I overreacted at Victor's. And the graveyard.

DaMage: I guess we should talk about that too.

Me: You were right. Kyle fucked up. Victor did what he had to.

DaMage: It's not as simple as Kyle fucking up.

Me: How was it more complicated? Because it didn't come through in Victor's story.

DaMage: You didn't read him well enough. Surprising, considering.

Me: Considering what?

DaMage: How many layers of lies you've survived on.

He ceased typing, dropped his head back on the pillow, and

faced me. "I'm sorry. I shouldn't have said that."

I shrugged. "It's true."

He frowned, and I returned to hacking into the safety of the laptop.

Me: How was it more complicated?

DaMage: I think Victor didn't let Kyle back into his life because he couldn't believe Kyle still loved him.

Me: The hell? Kyle clearly wanted to get back together.

DaMage: Kyle went over there and would have discovered Victor missing a leg, possibly angry and depressed. Victor would have interpreted any kindness—and love—as sympathy and guilt. He couldn't trust that Kyle still truly loved him. Victor never received those letters, either. In his mind, things ended badly, and suddenly, crippled from war, Kyle wants him back?

Suppressed emotion sheened Hunter's blue eyes. I gritted my teeth against an ache. We weren't entirely talking about Victor anymore, were we?

Carefully, I typed back.

Me: Is that what happened to you and Charlie?

His Adam's apple jutted. I gently pressed my arm against his, wanting him to feel okay to cry.

Wanting to let him know I cared.

But the words weren't unlocking between us.

Hunter laughed at himself, scrubbing his face. I pulled the laptop closer and typed again.

Me: You don't have to tell me. Sorry.

DaMage: Yes. That's how I felt after I . . . with Charlie.

"God, Hunter."

DaMage: It never would have lasted between us. No one wants to date this forever.

DaMage: It was easier to dump him first.

Hunter's pain stung me. I set our laptops aside and nuzzled into his side. Hunter dropped his head against mine and mindlessly played with my tank top.

"What your parents have. You want that."

His lips pressed against the corner of my forehead.

"That's why you need to save the gazebo."

Hope.

Hunter said nothing.

"I've decided I don't care for . . . surviving tonight," I murmured.

Hunter crushed me close. His laugh peppered softly against my temple.

"At least," I whispered, "not that kind of surviving."

I shuffled down into the cooler, untouched sheets and rearranged the pillows, while Hunter positioned himself facing me, one leg set over a body cushion.

Only our movements and soft breaths filled the space between us.

I carefully looped my leg around his pillow and felt the warmth of his leg against mine.

My forearm nestled against his; Hunter's pinkie twitched and I looped my finger around it.

His eyes shot to mine in the cozy glow. He lifted my hand to his mouth and grazed his lips over my knuckles.

I shuffled closer until our noses almost touched. Disentangling my fingers, I skated a light path over his bared neck. Hunter shivered, closing his eyes, and I did it again, zigzagging over his skin, touching new places, watching tiny hairs stand on end.

I skimmed the pad of my finger over the tips of those hairs and reveled in Hunter's sharp breath and jerky shiver. Arousal had me half-hard, but that wasn't my focus.

I drew a spiral over his shoulder to the small bird at his breast perched at the soft, darker skin surrounding his nipple. The wings were outstretched, and I traced every feather.

My finger sank over the hardened nub of his nipple and Hunter's breathing hitched. Through my thumbnail, I felt a pulse. Mine? Or his wild-banging heart?

Hunter curled an arm around my shoulder. Our eyes met, the seconds soft and intimate. I bumped my nose against his, another point of electricity between us.

I swallowed, and Hunter urged me nearer to him with a squeeze to my nape.

Our lips fit against each other's, ticklish and dry, and I gasped against him. He pressed into the kiss. Firm, warm, confident contact.

I held back from thrusting my tongue into his mouth, gently tugging at his nipple. Smiling against him.

"Marc . . ." Hunter's voice thrummed with emotion.

I shivered, and re-slotted our lips together, damp enough now to moisten them with my tongue.

Hunter moaned into my mouth, pulled back, and kissed me again.

His hand left my hair and dragged over my arm to my fingers teasing him. He steered me lower, cresting his ribcage to just above his belly button. "There."

"There?" My voice came out rough, croaky.

"It's extra sensitive for me."

I wasn't sure I completely understood. "Is this where sensation starts for you?"

His eyes held mine, and I saw him battle nervousness. "There aren't many intimate places I can share with someone I . . ." He cleared his throat. "Yes."

Our fingers shook as he steered me around the edges of where he could feel.

Sensing Hunter's vulnerability, I leaned in and kissed him, retracing the path he'd shown me. His moan broke against my lips and his body shuddered. "Do you like it softer, or harder?"

"This is perfect. You can touch me there however you want, Marc. Tender or rough, pinch or stroke."

"Really?"

"Yes."

I wriggled down, kissing his chin, his throat, his nipple.

"Marc?"

I flicked my tongue at the edge of his sensitivity and Hunter rolled onto his back. I helped shift his leg, parting enough to crawl between his thighs. I tongued my way over the path he'd shown me, across his muscled torso, tasting slightly salty skin.

Hunter's hands raked through my hair, tugging lightly where he was most sensitive. I breathed him in and kissed as many shivers out of him as I could.

"Oh." Hunter grunted, pulling me up against him.

His eyes glistened, lashes damp. "I've never shown anyone that before."

A powerful feeling surged through me, and Hunter tightened his hold around my waist. His breath hitched at my throat, and someone was murmuring Hunter's name. Me.

I slammed my eyes shut. He gripped my face and swept a tender kiss over my lips.

This was getting out of control.

Hunter shouldn't feel like this for me. I couldn't accept it.

Shouldn't. Accept. It.

Fuck.

CHAPTER THIRTEEN

Over breakfast—bowls of muesli and orange juice—Hunter called the number on Kyle Gable Green's card and organized a meeting for Friday.

"Great, yeah," I said, and gulped my drink. "We'll change his mind, and then Monday's plan to tear down the Gazebo will be moot."

Sunlight streamed through the kitchen window behind Hunter, fitting and beautiful, and it made my heart sick that I would have to end us.

Sooner than later—and before it got more complicated. I wanted him happily wrapped up with a good person who was worthy of him. Someone who had never spoken bad about him behind his back, or flipped him off, or sniggered at him . . .

Someone who didn't ruin beautiful things.

Except.

I also didn't want to let him go.

"What are you thinking about?" Hunter asked, brow hitching.

I dropped my spoon and cavalierly folded my arms. Bullshit flavored the tip of my tongue, and I swallowed it. I sighed, rippling the milk puddle in my bowl. "Last night."

Hunter paused. "Last night was especially memorable." His little smile into his bowl had my insides tearing.

Maybe . . .

What if I could be good enough? Worthy enough?

I wanted to be.

I could start by saving Hunter's Gazebo and promise of future love. Mine, if I was so lucky.

Desperate, I jumped to my feet and grabbed Kyle's card. Friday was two days too far away. I called his secretary back and plead for an earlier appointment. Today.

"He's busy in meetings all day."

"He must eat lunch."

She sighed down the line. "He has business meetings over lunch, too."

"Please, I only need five minutes."

"We'll see you on Friday, good day." She hung up. I cursed and shoved my phone into my pocket.

Hunter finished washing our dishes and turned his low-key amusement on me. "It's one night. There's still time."

"I'm impatient, remember?" Especially about whether I had a chance with Hunter.

I collapsed onto his navy, cushion-covered couch.

A curious-looking Hunter wearing a DaMage T-shirt rolled to my feet. I wriggled my toes at the cute dimples deepening in his shaven cheeks.

He massaged the balls of my feet as he mused, "I have a camera . . ."

"Huh?"

"A really good camera. Fantastic lens."

"Okay . . ."

A cheeky glint hit his eye. "And a white van with tinted windows . . ."

I pushed onto my elbows, snickering. "What are you saying, we kidnap him?"

"Or follow him. Catch him on the way to lunch."

"We don't even know where he lives."

Hunter shrugged. "Geek Force God, remember?"

I swung off the couch and grabbed his laptop from the bedroom. "Let's do this."

WE PARKED across the road from Gable Green Enterprises, a mini mansion of family offices, under an oak teeming with squirrels racing around its sunbaked trunk. It was like living in Utopia —sometimes I wouldn't mind waking up a squirrel.

Hunter had the window open, camera trained toward the house. "I see movement upstairs, no idea who it is."

He settled the camera on his lap. "It's not quite eleven, so we have time."

"I know it sucks skipping econ"—especially because of my promise to Ben—"but this feels enormously important . . ."

Hunter watched me with kindness I couldn't absorb. He gestured to the glovebox. "There are snacks."

I passed him a Coke and a Snickers. He ripped the bar open and bit into it with a happy moan. I greedily accepted the next offered bite. "I thought you were careful with your diet?"

"Exceptions for stalking dates."

"We should do more stalking dates."

Hunter laughed, light and carefree. I wondered if I should have implicitly promised more dates. My stomach twisted on the chocolate.

"Regardless," Hunter said. "I'll burn it all off tonight at basketball practice."

"Guess that means you're busy. Which is good. Fine. I can't crash at your place every night. Besides, I should face my uncle." I nibbled at the Snickers bar. "At least change into my own underwear."

Hunter palmed my upper thigh. "You can wear my underwear any day of the week."

"Some might say that's disgusting." I handed him back the chocolate and stole his Coke. "I say it's disgustingly romantic."

Watching the squirrels, Hunter snickered and bit into the bar. "Get used to it."

"Because you love cheesiness?"

"Because I love"—he glanced at me then instantly back at the offices—"cheesiness."

The air throbbed with intimacy. Feelings from last night bubbled in my chest so hard, I was about to puke.

I sat on my shaking hands and reached deep for all the bullshit I could use to shield me from the hope and the dumb aching need . . .

When Kyle left his mansion offices, we trailed him to a French restaurant. Hunter manned the getaway van while I cut our K off before he reached the frosted-glass door.

Kyle snapped to a startled halt.

"Mr. Gable Green," I rushed out, aware I should get to the point quickly. "I'm Marc from the *Scribe*. I would like to ask you a few questions about the removal of Lover's Loop Gazebo."

He rocked back in his loafers and clasped his hands behind his back. "Excuse me?"

"I'm part of a large, growing number of students and alumni that are actively working to stop the dismantling of this historic landmark."

"I'm about to meet investors for lunch."

"I'm only asking for your voice to reverse this decision. The Gazebo holds immeasurable sentimental value."

He slammed his eyes shut and I read the pain wracking his body. "I have lunch to get to."

I caught hold of his crushed soul and decided to take a risk. "I found your letters to Victor Albacore."

He staggered back and I instinctively grabbed his arm, worried he'd stumble into the gutter. "You okay?"

He pulled free. "You pop out of nowhere and rip into my past. No, I'm not okay."

I was losing him. My voice grew desperate. "Why are you insisting the Gazebo be removed?"

"The university is updating outdoor campus facilities."

I blurted after him, "It hurts, doesn't it? To walk by and remember the past, how much you loved him."

He froze. "I have to ask you to please leave."

I stepped back, heat prickling my eyes. "You need to do something."

He looked sad. Older, and gray with emotion. "I am. I'm having it taken down."

When he pulled open the frosted door, I called after him, "You're making a mistake."

HUNTER and I parted ways on campus to our respective lectures, and I ended up planting myself in the front row of History 321 alongside Tyler. Fidgety and frustrated, I wanted company.

He jerked his head up. "You look like a walking natural disaster."

I shoved a hand through my hair to tame it. "Kinda true. Hey, did you take econ notes?"

Tyler opened his email on his laptop. "What's your address?"

"Could you send them to Hunter, too?"

He stared at me. "Oh. Are you two . . .?"

"If I play my cards right?"

A flash of disappointment hit his eyes. "Okay, sure. Your addresses?"

I told him and he sent them to us. After class, we had coffee at the union café and I realized there was a lot more to Tyler than I'd once thought. We shared a love of football that had a dreamy look crossing his face, and he used to run cross country, too. Maybe I could get back into running, save my abs. We could run together maybe. He was working with Uncle Ben on sports writing, too. Ambition. Interests.

"I'm not just an IT nerd."

Even though the day had kinda sucked, I smiled. Tyler was a good guy I could be friends with. I imagined Hunter's parents and their tuna sandwiches, and it gave me stupid fuzzy feelings.

"Know any kind, single guys?" Tyler tossed out there.

"Not really." I took a gulp of coffee.

"No distant cousin or neighbor—or hey, lonely uncle?"

I spat my coffee on the table.

Tyler laughed. "I take it that's a yes to the uncle?"

I wiped up the coffee mess. "Yes, but no. You and Chief Benedict? Never in a million years."

"Wait. *Chief Benedict* is your uncle?"

"Why is this so shocking to everyone?"

Tyler frowned. "Sorry, say that again?"

I spoke more clearly, and Tyler grinned. "He is hot."

"He's taken." Maybe. If I hadn't ruined that.

We agreed to have coffee again soon. Tyler happily suggested Hunter join us, and the invitation had a weird effect on me. I couldn't stop grinning and I moved quicker too. I was itching to do something. Change K's mind.

I wrote my article and sent it for Hunter's approval before I sent it to editing.

He replied quickly that he loved it, and could he pass it on to his parents?

I rolled my eyes. "Of course."

Hannah shot quirky sideways glances at me from her desk, like she'd been doing all afternoon.

I hung up, leaned back in my chair, and caught her eye. "You all right, Hannah?"

She blushed and slung herself at Hunter's desk, pen and paper in hand. "So, you and Hunter are boyfriends?"

I lurched upright. "Did he tell you that?"

She frowned. "No. I just . . . assumed?"

I relaxed. "You know the story with assuming . . ."

"Oh." I understood her disappointment. I also was battling mixed feelings about the idea.

I nodded to her paper. "What're you working on?"

"I've been working up the guts all evening to ask if you'd review my draft?"

"Hand it over."

Her smile of gratitude radiated warmly over me. Deserved, I wasn't sure. But I liked it.

Her article was good, her voice fresh. Other than a few small queries, I had little to critique. She beamed all the way back to her desk.

Uncle Ben caught my eye from his office. Too busy working with students, he only nodded. At the end of the day, he caught me leaving for home.

"Marc."

Hannah and Liam were nearby. Liam was clicking the end of his pen. "Yeah?"

"Jason caught an earlier flight and I'm picking him up from the airport tonight. We won't be home until late."

I nodded dumbly. "I was gonna . . . hang out online anyway."

I started to leave and paused when he spoke—low, for my ears only. "I wouldn't have changed anything, you know."

I left, battling a blurry phone screen as I typed him a message.

Me: Maybe we can do dinner, the three of us, tomorrow?

Uncle Ben: Let's do that.

AT HOME, I brought in the mail, stopping abruptly when I saw a letter addressed to me from Jack.

Shit. Did I open it? Burn the damn thing?

I stuffed the letter into my desk drawer and sank into my chair. I stared between the Archie tin and my folder of lettered apologies.

What if Jack's letter was an apology?

Would I be able to forgive him?

With that heavy question hanging over my head, I opened Demon-Slayage and tried to lose myself. But it wasn't the same without DaMage.

The answer was no, goddammit. I wouldn't forgive Jack. He wasn't Hunter's attacker, but he may as well have been. Never in a million years would I forgive anyone who hurt Hunter.

How dare I expect a different outcome for myself.

CLOSE TO TEN o'clock at night, a knock at my basement door startled me. I leaped out of bed where I'd been staring at the ceiling listening to Bach. Air whooshed inside in my hurry to open.

Hunter sat with a broad smile and bright cheeks, his hair like a fucking halo. The subtle arch of his eyebrow, the confident sweep of his shoulders, and his *Knight in Shining Armor* T-shirt under his jacket. Giddiness made me dizzy, and I gripped the door.

Hunter drummed his fingers over his wheels. "My place feels super empty without you. So"—he lifted a backpack—"I brought everything I need for a slumber party."

I stepped aside. "Fuck, yeah."

Everything needed for a slumber party meant not only pills and catheters and clean underwear, but also limes, mint, and Bacardi.

I prepared a mojito pitcher and smuggled it with two glasses into my basement. Hunter lay draped lengthwise on my couch and had shucked his shoes, jeans, and jacket. Happy socks decorated with pictures of knights were pulled halfway up his ankles. The geek had dressed to match.

I smirked and dragged a small table over for our mojito pitcher. I stripped out of my jeans. My socks weren't as fun, but I didn't care. "Room on that couch for me?"

I mirrored Hunter's sitting position, legs stretched over the cushions. "Can I . . ." I gestured to his legs.

"Sure."

I settled them between mine, and Hunter passed me a mojito. We sipped in soft silence, electricity rippling between us, the weight of his heels on my lap stirring me half-hard.

"Tell me something," Hunter murmured.

"This music we're listening to? I dig it."

"Not surprised."

"Really?"

"I distinctly remember you humming Chopin's Funeral March, why wouldn't you listen to Bach's Toccata and Fugue in D minor?"

I straightened. "You're into classical music too," I said accusingly.

"This one sounds particularly tense."

The top tracks were playing on loop, and this had been the song I'd listened to before Hunter arrived. It had felt like each beat had been plucked from my gut. I glanced at Hunter's studying gaze and took a large gulp of mojito.

I wanted so badly.

Could I have him?

Hunter set his glass down and gestured to take mine. He curled a finger. "Come here."

He smelled like soap and shampoo. Sadly no traces of sweat remained from basketball practice. His wide chest cushioned my back comfortably as I settled snug against him.

"Da-da-dum-dum," Hunter hummed, lips hovering against my ear.

I squirmed on his lap, shivering at the tickle and the accompanying tension.

He looped his arms around my waist and kissed my neck. I turned my head, clumsily snatching his lips with mine.

"Your lips are perfect," Hunter said, our noses bumping.

I met his mouth in a hot, desperate kiss, body and mind pleading for more.

I wriggled around, straddling him, consuming his mouth, hands roaming through his hair, down his neck, over his biceps. My hard dick pushed against the fabric of my boxers, aching for touch, and Hunter freed me, curling a firm grip around me, pumping slowly.

My breath hitched into his mouth and Hunter smiled.

"Shall we take this to your bed?"

I scrambled off him, perched at the lip of the couch. "Arms around my neck!"

Hunter laughed loudly, charmed by my enthusiasm. I piggy-backed him to my bed where he rolled in the tangled sheets and pulled his boxers over his ass. I swatted him away and drew the boxers off his legs with my mouth.

He watched on his elbows. "I'm leaving your socks on," I said, crookedly balancing on my mattress as I stripped my underwear.

"What if I only want one knight on me?"

I stilled. Butterflies needing to fly free balled in my throat. I kneeled and stripped him of each sock. I wondered if Hunter's growing smile mirrored the one eating my face.

"In my bag," Hunter said. "I have condoms and lube."

I found them and settled them at the pillow next to Hunter's head as I flattened my hard body against his. My dick rubbed at the base of his stomach and I shuffled upward so it hit Hunter's line of sensation.

"You're warm and hard," he said into another kiss.

I grabbed his hands and stretched them over his head, using his resistance to thrust against him. "So fucking hard for you."

Hunter greedily grabbed my hair, pushing me into a tongue-thrusting kiss. It pulled at my roots, but I didn't care because Hunter made a soft moan and his eyes fluttered.

We kissed and kissed. I rubbed myself against him, perfectly content to come like this.

Hunter broke the kiss and smoothed his fingers over my jaw. Our eyes locked, fraught with electricity that zipped from my scalp to my toes. Hunter parted his lips and closed them again, his chest rising and falling under me.

"What?" I whispered.

"I . . ." He glanced sideways toward the red carnation that still thrived in water.

The ball at his throat jutted, and I turned his face to mine. "Tell me?"

"I don't want you to come like this." His jaw twitched determinedly. "I want you to come inside me."

He regarded me quietly as I struggled to find my voice. "Are you, um, sure?"

"Yes."

My dick pulsed hard at the offer, but not as much as my heart. I ran fingers over his jaw to the soft skin below his ear, and I stroked as I searched for the right answer.

His hand closed around the back of mine. "Only if you want to, Marc."

He kissed me softly. My body kickstarted, powered by a billion nerve endings begging me to say yes.

I wasn't sure that I should. Not until I was certain I could be good enough for Hunter. I'd never done this, and it'd been a long time for him, and his first time without feeling sensation . . .

"I want to," I said. I failed to move the "but" past the lump in my throat.

Hunter kissed me and I shivered as I melted into it.

I gave in to Hunter's hopeful blue eyes.

"I want to," I said, and shoved away my concerns. "I really want to."

We kissed again, chuckling into each other. I straddled him. "How do we do this?"

"With humor. It might not be graceful." He paused. "Maybe we should forgo the funeral march?"

I snickered and reached to switch the music off.

Our breaths sounded loud and my leg shifting sounded like Velcro. I winced. "Maybe the funeral march after all?"

Hunter laughed and pulled me down. Gravity chased me with a rush of delicious shivers, and I wriggled down kissing a figure eight around his nipples.

Hunter impatiently grabbed the lube and tapped the cool plastic against my shoulder. "More of that once you're in me."

I settled myself between his legs and poured a glob of it over my fingers. "How will I know if it's hurting you?"

"I prepared myself before coming over here. Stretched myself. I should be fine. But . . . use lots of lube and go slowly."

Sex was a messy, awkward, inelegant event in the best cases, but it was also intense and fun. It was all this with Hunter, and way fucking more.

It was vulnerable and shy and intimate—and most of all brave. I manhandled Hunter, plunged my lubed fingers into his ass, lifted his legs onto my shoulders, and he opened himself to every touch. Watched me do it, eyes connecting with mine, bottom lip pressed between his teeth.

I turned my head and kissed his inner thigh, holding his gaze.

We both shivered as I lined up my latexed cock. I nudged against his entrance, moaning at the promise of breaching him, and halted. I needed Hunter to feel this too, somehow.

I lowered his legs and sank against him. I touched my left hand lightly against his. "When I'm holding your hand tight, that's when I'm deep in you."

He surged up for a kiss and I kissed him back, fumbling for the right angle. When I found it, I pressed forward.

I slowly curled my fingers between his and squeezed with the intensity his body was squeezing me. I braced my weight on my other arm, shaking with strain as I waited for his body to accept me. "You feel incredible, Hunter," I whispered.

He watched my face, his expression slack with joy, lips curved gently.

I couldn't hold back. I pulled back and pushed into him again, groaning, swearing. He felt so good, slick and tight, and—I thrust into him again and again—"Fuuuuuuck."

With every thrust, I pumped his hand and he met my pumps with his own.

I wanted to explore all his sensitive spots, but reaching and holding myself . . . I sank against him, sweaty and wriggly as I nuzzled his neck.

He groaned and I doubled my efforts to make him feel amazing. Like he made me feel.

Hunter's free hand roamed my back, pressing me against him, and slid into my hair. He whispered against my ear. "More. Lower. Right there. Suck hard."

His groan rippled over my neck. Our chests lifted and rose together as we found our rhythm, and it enhanced our connection a thousand times over.

My toes pressed against the tops of his feet and I vaguely realized he was taller than me. Taller, broader, stronger—and absolutely divine.

I swiveled my hips, mirroring it with the sweep of my thumb over his.

Close. I was so close.

I snagged his other hand and gently knotted our fingers together, thrusts urgent and messy. I rocked harder and faster into him, hand slowly closing around Hunter's like a vice.

My orgasm throttled through me, hitting in hard, fast pulsing waves that went on and on.

I whimpered against his neck and Hunter clutched my hands through it. His thigh muscles involuntarily contracted, and I collapsed onto him, kissing his throat. "You came too?"

I felt the wet patch against my lower stomach.

I shifted for him to see. "You must have really massaged my prostate."

I hid my face against his shoulder. "Did you feel it in your chest?"

He shifted and I slipped out of him, rolling against his side. My hand sank to the hummingbird over his heart. "Yeah," he said. "I felt it in my chest."

I tucked my face against his armpit. "That was impossibly sexy."

Once I'd discarded the condom and cleaned the come from us, I shut out all the lights but the one at my bedside and curled against him.

Hunter smacked my ass as he kissed me. I slipped my tongue over his bottom lip, holding his gaze—and maybe a million butterflies.

He pulled back, breathlessly laughing, and I knew I wanted this to last. Fuck, I'd save the Gazebo, I'd fix things with everyone I'd ever wronged, and I'd beg the universe to let me be good enough for this.

I traced the hummingbird at Hunter's chest and reveled in the sensation of his lips brushing my forehead.

But across the room on my desk sat pages and pages detailing my worst behavior.

Unsent letters of apology tormented what should have been the best sleep of my life.

CHAPTER FOURTEEN

Hunter: Want to sleep at my place?

Me: I'm having dinner with my uncle and Jason . . .

Hunter: Oh, in that case definitely come over after.

I laughed and groaned, deleting my reply over and over.

Hunter: I can only stare at three bouncing dots so long . . .

Me: I'm afraid I might be in a mood.

Hunter: I know what to do in that case.

Me: Funny.

Hunter: I try.

Me: Hey, did you look into that rental agency? I said I'd move out by the end of the month, and I haven't looked for anything.

Hunter: Maybe we can discuss this tonight, face to face?

I rubbed the end of my phone over my forehead to quell the sickening giddiness.

Me: Sure. Could you send me your lemon pasta recipe?

I KEPT LOOKING at the clock. Half an hour before Uncle Ben said he'd be home from his day out with Jason. I hadn't heard them come in last night, nor had I seen them so far today. The scent of Jason's aftershave lingered in the air and his purple suitcases lay in Uncle Ben's room.

Every other time he'd stayed, he'd dropped his things into the guest room. Guess there was no need for hiding anymore.

I stared at the ingredients on the counter and followed Hunter's live stream instructions. I loved that he'd be eating the same meal, a connection between us when we couldn't be together.

"Why are you running the pasta under water?" Hunter said, squinting from the screen.

"Rinsing it."

"It's not rice."

"Are you fucking serious right now?"

"Holy shit," Hunter laughed. "You've been rinsing pasta your whole life?"

"I thought it was the same as rice. To clean the dust particles and . . . germs?"

"Just a moment." Hunter disappeared, and his kitchen shook in time with a bountiful laugh.

"I can still hear you."

Hunter returned. "You are adorable."

"Piss off."

He grinned into the camera and I might have grinned back.

Following his recipe, I had dinner ready in twenty minutes. The front door slammed and raised voices came from the entryway.

"Why won't you admit it?" That sounded like a wounded Jason.

I stopped tossing the pasta and lemon sauce and listened.

"It's not the time to admit anything," Uncle Ben said sharply.

"Seriously? Because I flew from Germany to talk about this."

"And you have a return flight next Monday."

"Yes, but—"

Uncle Ben cut him off. "I told you the truth: I don't mind you seeing other people."

"You were supposed to be seeing others too."

"Does it make a difference?"

"Yes!" Jason's pain and frustration echoed through the house. "It makes a huge fucking difference."

"Can we pause this conversation? Marc wants to join us for dinner."

"I should be good at pausing my feelings. God knows I've been doing it for years."

"What?" Uncle Ben sounded quieter.

"Ever since Marc moved in with you."

I tensed, shutting my eyes. Hunter moved on screen, frowning. Could he hear Uncle Ben and Jason too? They were certainly loud enough.

Jason sighed and I could imagine him sinking against the front door staring at his folded arms. "I always knew he had to come first. I understood that. He was only a boy, he needed you and stability, but letting you go after seventeen years of following each other around the world hurt, Harry. This house, your job, it was meant to be temporary. Sitting next to an empty seat on what was meant to be our flight to Europe, our next adventure. I know it was selfish, we had a good run, but every time we called, I had to hold my tears in so you knew I had your back, that I accepted your decision."

"You never wanted kids—God knows we fought about that—and Marc wasn't easy on you or me at the beginning." Shame washed through me and I stared at the pasta. Hunter gently cleared his throat, and I couldn't stand him seeing me. Eyes blurry, I ended our call and pocketed the phone.

Uncle Ben murmured, "I could never have asked you to stay."

A sniff. "Maybe you should have asked me anyway."

"Jason, honey. Ballet is your life. You had opportunities few ever do. I couldn't ask you to give them up."

Jason sobbed and my throat ached. The enormity of what Uncle Ben had given up . . .

Shaking, I moved to the hall. Jason's head was buried against Uncle Ben's chest.

My step hitched, and they sharply looked over.

Uncle Ben frowned and I cut him off before he could address me.

"I cursed you, I hit you, I broke your car window." Strong, salt-and-pepper haired Jason blinked as a tear rolled down his high cheekbone. His pouty lips pressed together. "I hated him, then, I laughed at him." I forced myself to meet Uncle Ben's eyes. "You gave up your dreams for that, but you never should have. You should have sent me into care."

Uncle Ben gripped Jason harder, frowning hard at me. "Don't, Marc. This isn't about you."

I scoffed, hard. "Who are you fooling?"

"This situation is difficult and *not your fault*, do you hear me?"

I didn't believe him for a second. "You know what? Dinner's ready. I'm leaving."

"Hey, hey. We can do dinner together, we can fix this."

I laughed hollowly and Jason shuddered in Uncle Ben's arms, like he did back when I was an asshole. Maybe I still was an asshole. "No, we can't. You guys can. Talk to each other. Start over, knowing I'm not in your way anymore." I held Uncle Ben's eye. "Admit your true feelings."

I twisted on my heel and stalked toward the basement staircase.

"Come back here, Marc."

I ignored him.

His footsteps pounded against the floor as he chased after me. "Wait."

I whirled around. "What? What could I possibly do to change the last six years?"

He stopped. "You can't."

"See?" I held in the sting.

"Please stay."

"Don't you see? Standing here listening to your and Jason's pain, knowing that I'm the reason . . . It's screwing with me, okay?"

Jason came up behind Uncle Ben and settled a hand on his shoulder. "Let him have his space, Harry. Please?"

Uncle Ben folded a step toward Jason, and I rushed the last steps into the basement.

———

PACING THE BASEMENT, I stuffed Cheetos into my mouth trying to get myself under control. No easy feat while hearing the murmur of continued argument upstairs. With orange fingers, I opened my folder of unsent letters, determined to fix shit, but . . . look how well things had gone tonight.

Frustrated and apparently willing to make things worse, I opened Jack's letter.

Might as well clean up all the crap at once.

Jill,

Look, this isn't me asking for forgiveness or whatever but maybe our talk got nasty.

I was remembering our old antics, and the truth is you used to ask me if what we were doing was a good idea. You'd give me a look, like maybe I was going too far.

I guess . . . I talked a lot about you being like me, but maybe you're not.

Yeah, that's it for now,

Jack

I stared at the words, long and hard. Perhaps they should be comforting. *You're not like me.* But I read between the lines: *You thought whatever we were doing or saying wasn't right, and you did and said it anyway.*

You're worse.

My phone had been buzzing and again I ignored it. I fucked about the room, stubbing my toe as I kicked the couch. Laughing through the pain, I opened my laptop and dove into old Demon-Slayage chats.

September

DaMage: What do you think love is?

Me: Not a question I expected . . .

DaMage: Confession: I'm tipsy.

Me: Confession: I wish I could see what that looks like.

DaMage: Looks like me, sprawled on my couch, listening to Al Green's "Let's Stay Together."

Me: Good song.

DaMage: So what do you think?

Me: Nice image.

DaMage: About love.

Me: Dude, I'm the wrong person to ask. The last guy I crushed on . . . it couldn't have ended worse.

DaMage: I think love is comfortable silence and giving in to laughs at silly puns and patiently putting up with each other's crap.

Me: What are you drinking? May I have some?

DaMage: *snort.* Good lyrics, these. You should listen.

I hadn't listened to it then, but I found it on Spotify and played it as I checked Hunter's numerous messages asking if I was okay. I blinked back overwhelming emotion and wiped away the stray splotches that landed on my phone.

Me: Thanks for the pasta recipe. It was delicious.

Hunter: You sure you're good?

Me: 'Course.

Hunter: Coming around?

Me: You bet.

I packed a bag, stuffing the Archie tin and my letters inside. Not sure what my plan was with the latter, but I followed my instinct.

One Uber ride later, I was eating Hunter's lemon pasta leftovers from the pot at the kitchen table. He watched me devour it, head cocked, fingers drumming the table. His gaze dropped to the orange-stained cuff of my sleeve. Damn Cheetos.

I gulped my mouthful, a funny lurch in my stomach. Hunter read right through me.

"How were your, um, classes?" I said.

"Fine."

"All your studying done?"

His eyes narrowed with a frown, and he wheeled around the table, trapping me in the kitchen. His jaw was hard, no sign of a dimple anywhere. Goosebumps rippled over me.

Oh, fuck, he knew something was up. Why did he have to be so intuitive?

I grabbed the backpack that I'd tossed on the table. "I should hang this up."

I started to round him and he cut me off with a sharp swivel of his chair. "Just a moment." His deep voice held a note of command and then his eyes softened, filled with patience. "You said you'd be in a mood, yet you're hiding it."

I cast a panicked gaze toward the pot. "Did I tell you I really love this dish?"

"You implied you ate already."

"It's the parmesan that gives it oomph."

"It's the lemon rind, but the combo is good."

"Lemon rind, yeah. Delicious. Should we do some Demon-Slayage?" I hefted my bag. "Got my laptop."

"I overheard things, Marc. You were visibly shaking. You hung up without goodbye."

"Shoulda said goodbye. Oops," I gave him an apologetic grin.

"That's not the part I care about."

I slung my bag over my shoulder and rubbed the strap. "There's nothing to worry about."

Hunter's frown deepened.

"I'm good. Totally awesome. The best evah."

"You're bullshitting me." Hunter leaned forward and whispered, "You're bullshitting yourself." He added softly, "I thought we were past that."

A sad twitch jerked his jaw, and I felt a million pained twitches of my own. They kept growing, multiplying. Panic squeezed my lungs.

"What do you want from me, Hunter?" It came out a gravelly plea.

He took a deep breath, like he was nervous. "Isn't it obvious?"

I paced the five feet between the table and the stove, my socks gliding against the tile. I plucked off a leaf of basil hanging next to Peter the pepper plant. Its aroma spiced the air as I squished it between my fingers.

"I can't," I blurted and slapped my basil hand over my traitorous mouth.

"Can't be boyfriends?" He held my eye. "Or can't move in with me?"

Oh, fuck. "Both. Either."

Frustration and confusion rose in the flush of Hunter's cheeks. He frowned down at his legs, and I wanted to cry.

I shook my head vehemently.

"No, no, that's not . . ." I ripped open my bag and shakily pulled out my unsent letters. Every horrible thing I'd ever done I'd written into its pages, and the idea of giving it to Hunter to read made me sick. "You deserve someone better, Hunter."

"You think I haven't heard those words before?" he said sourly. "Think I don't know what that means?"

"It doesn't mean whatever you're thinking," I snap.

"Then talk to me. Explain."

"I'm afraid you won't like me after."

His laugh was dry, hollow. "Is it worse than us fighting right now? Worse than breaking my . . ."

A shuddering sniff escaped me, and Hunter's anger quelled.

He spoke softly, "What's going on?"

Shakily, I pressed my letters into his hands. Deep down I'd known I would pass them to Hunter tonight. "Read that. Everything."

I hid myself in his bedroom while he read my letters. I curled into a ball in the middle of his bed, breathing in the scent of Hunter on his pillows.

Twenty minutes later, the door groaned open and wheels rolled over the smooth floors.

Hunter muscled himself from his chair into the bed, where he positioned himself on his side and patted the mattress for me to mirror him. His face was serious, and I was going to throw up. This was it. The last conversation.

My pulse pounded in anticipation and I slid onto my side.

It took everything to bear his intense stare, and I wanted to beg him to rip the Band-Aid off quick.

Hunter pressed his palm against the side of my face and spoke softly. "You really do have shit for brains if you think this changes anything."

I pulled back from him frowning. "Did you read all the letters? Liam's? Uncle Ben's? Jason's? *Yours?*"

"I read them all. And Jack's letter to you."

I bowed my head. "And?"

"That Jill was a real shithead."

An embarrassed sob hammered at my throat and I squeezed it down, my voice tiny, "Yes."

"But the Marc before me?" His fingertips trailed over the curve of my shaven jaw to my Adam's apple. "Not so much."

I clung to impossibly rising hope. "How can you know that for sure?" I gestured in the direction of the kitchen. "I still lie."

"You shield yourself. You struggle to let go, to be completely vulnerable." Hunter thought quietly. "But you're trying. With me, you're trying and that means something. It . . ."

"It . . .?"

"It makes me want to tear down the last of my shields too."

"You have any left?"

Hunter chuckled. "Why do you think I spend so much time on Demon-Slayage as DaMage—invisible 'd'?"

Hearing Hunter speak his online name came as a punch. He didn't pronounce it Daaaa Mage like I had in my head. He pronounced it "damaged." The horrifying implications of it tore at my twisted stomach. I sat up, shaking.

"Damaged?" I pushed him onto his back and climbed onto him. I stared down at his deep blue eyes and spoke, sad, angry. "That's how you think of yourself?" I thought of his mage character. Tall and agile, he could work magic and heal the sick. It all became clear. "You play when you want to escape your reality?"

He shifted under me. "Yes. At least, that's how it started." He grabbed a handful of my shirt and pulled me down, face to face. "Until I met you, Fawkes."

He pronounced it "fucks," exactly as I had imagined it from day one. Chosen after my favorite, most overused word, to symbolize that whatever I touched, I fucked up. Hunter knew it. Because he was smart. Because he was intuitive.

Because he had been doing the same.

My breath was ragged with emotion against his lips as Hunter surged up and kissed me, his mouth hard and needy.

I pushed into it, tongue pushing deep, sliding slickly against his. The kiss was frustrated and passionate, and Hunter moaned into it, the vibrations pulsing all the way to my toes.

Hunter shoved me off him and dragged himself over me. My knees helped angle his legs between mine. His heavy warm weight sank against me, and fucking tears leaked down my cheeks, because this wasn't goodbye. Wasn't the last time we would do this.

This was the first time. No lies, no shield between us.

Our sex was raw and frantic, slow and intimate, and I wanted to shout how much he meant to me. I shivered after I came, and Hunter's soft mouth met mine, kissing me through this crazy, unbearable lightness.

I sucked his throat and whispered how much I loved sex with him in his ear. He sneezed, and I laughed, so carefree and ridiculously hopeful.

I absorbed every detail of Hunter's face, how straight his lashes were, the sexy blush from our passion pinking his cheek, his throat, his mussed hair. "You know that thing you want from me, Hunter?"

"Being my boyfriend?"

I kissed his chin. "Ask me again on Monday?"

He faced me. "Why Monday?"

I whispered, "I have a mission." *I want to feel worthy of you.*

Shrewd eyes crinkled at the edges. "You want to save the Gazebo."

"I need to."

Hunter brushed the hair off my face. "As long as I—your wise, ass-saving mage—can be by your side."

I snorted, smacking the back of his head, and pushed him into another kiss.

CHAPTER FIFTEEN

I was nervous over breakfast. It'd take time to understand these new feelings and accept they were allowed. It was strangely surreal, and sometimes I froze, a past memory barreling into me that I hadn't admitted in the letters. Was there something else I'd forgotten that would change Hunter's mind?

Hunter, reading my thoughts, covered my hand and squeezed. Warm and sure.

He drove us to campus and we went to class and sat side by side in the atrium. I barely heard a word the lecturer said, so aware of Hunter next to me. How would it feel to announce to everyone he was my boyfriend? To have Hunter clasp the back of my leg in public, claiming me as his?

Giddiness swept through me. Fuck.

I caught Red Jeans's curious glance and whispered intimately in Hunter's ear. Hunter whispered back in mine. "Sure, I'll have coffee with you after. Done marking your territory, Marc?"

I smiled against his ear. "Not even close."

I WAS FEELING like I should be alone in a bathroom cubicle. My insides were liquid with hope and it wasn't pretty.

Twelve-thirty sharp, Hunter and I were ushered into our scheduled meeting with Kyle Gable Green.

We entered a large room lined with dark bookshelves. Sunshine stamped blocks of light over the plush carpet, and a huge mahogany desk filled the space to our left. Behind it, Kyle rose in acknowledgement. He appeared—for seventy—like he ran marathons and forewent sugar. His wide smile waned, replaced by painful panic in his eyes.

He helped me remove one of the two high-back chairs and Hunter rolled next to me.

Kyle stiffly offered water. I accepted and liquid plopped unevenly into my glass.

"I was trying to place you the last time we met," Kyle said, looking at me. "You were the one treating your friend so disgracefully."

I recalled the moment in the gallery where I'd tossed sparkling wine over Hunter's lap, and heated.

Hunter cleared his throat. "You misunderstood the scene, sir. My . . . friend was saving my dignity."

"Your dignity?"

"I had an accident."

"Ah," Kyle said, understanding. "You're from *Scribe*, and you're here to convince me to save your gazebo. I'm afraid you're wasting your time."

I lifted the glass of water to my lips. "I'm not convinced that's the case."

Kyle's brows rose.

"See," I said after a refreshing sip, "Hunter and I were chatting about you last night, and we made some, quite frankly, remarkable realizations."

"Realizations." He cast a suspicious gaze between us.

I winked at Hunter, and his dimple popped. "We became aware of rather intriguing facts."

Kyle stirred on his chair. "Facts?"

"Yes, and we decided not to press you on the Gazebo today."

Confusion deepened the shadows around his eyes. "Then why are you here?"

Hunter lifted the Archie tin from his lap. He slid it toward Kyle Gable Green, whose face drained of color. His mouth parted in shock, and he tentatively touched the tin. "You really did find my letters."

"You know where, too."

He carefully opened the tin that Hunter had repaired.

I cleared my throat. "They were heartbreaking and beautiful."

Kyle lifted a letter out and read his words, voice gruff, soaked with memory and emotion.

"February, nineteen-seventy-three. Dear V, I've had it with this stupid war. With this stupid world. You're halfway across the world, fighting, making friends and losing them, and I do nothing but organize petitions in a fruitless effort stop the insanity and bring you home.

"I visited your sister yesterday. Her belly was swollen, close to her due date, and she shook as she told me her husband had died, that she had to move out of her rental. I went to our Gazebo and buckled into soul-wrenching sobs.

"I want you back. Even if you never forgive me. Just knowing you're living a long, happy life is all that matters.

"All my prayers, K."

Kyle shut his eyes briefly, then steeled his emotions. "This was written a long time ago."

I knew this tactic, and it wouldn't work on me. "I know you still care for him."

"You have no idea what you're talking about." He rose. "I think that wraps this meeting up, thank you."

"You will thank us," I said, leaning in, "because Hunter and I did a little geek-forcing. See, I've been thinking about moving out of my uncle's basement, and I asked Hunter to help me. We'd visited Victor's place and heard about what a fantastic rental agency he had. How he hadn't had a rent raise in years." Hunter seamlessly took over.

"Victor said when he returned from war, he rented a place through an agency called True Property Management. The prices for similar properties were astronomically more expensive than what the Albacores are paying. I hunted around and discovered something curious."

Hunter winked at me and I resumed, "True Property Management is owned by Gable Green Enterprises. It is you. You are Victor's landlord. You've kept his rent low. Not only his, also his sister's, and his sister's daughter's. You've been quietly taking care of the Albacore family since," I looked at Hunter, "when was it, honey?"

Hunter whipped his head toward mine, lips hopping. "1973, love."

The endearment shivered through me and I chomped down on a grin. I met Kyle's saddened gaze. "You helped Victor's sister find a place to live when she was pregnant while Victor was at war, and when he came home, you helped him too. You have been helping him—my guess, in many ways—forever."

The silence that followed was thick and Kyle rubbed his chest. His voice crackled. "He never would have accepted help if he knew it came from me. Are you here to negotiate the Gazebo for your silence?"

I frowned. "What?"

"That's your hand, isn't it? You'll tell Victor unless I stop the redesign of Lover's Loop."

I rubbed my forehead.

Kyle Gable Green picked up his phone and scrolled through his contacts.

All we'd have to do was keep quiet, and our gazebo—Hunter and Uncle Ben's gazebo—

would be saved.

I should have shut up, not exclaimed vehemently, "The fuck?"

Kyle's eyes shot to mine. Same with Hunter's.

"You are still in love with him!"

Kyle set down his phone. "Your point?"

"Give him those letters. Tell him your secrets yourself."

"I vowed to look after him."

"Excuse me, but what the actual fuck?"

Hunter choked and coughed into his fist, but I didn't care for propriety.

I continued, "You still have many years left. Don't drown in miscommunication. Talk."

His stubborn jaw twitched, but it was only to hold back the water building in his eyes. "Do I have your promise you won't share your findings with any Albacores or anyone else? Your gazebo is at stake."

Yes. That was the right answer.

Saving the gazebo was my mission to prove I was good enough to be Hunter's boyfriend.

What if it were Hunter and me distanced by war and past transgressions? If it were Hunter who had cast me out of his life?

Because he was afraid I'd break his heart first?

Afraid I didn't truly love him?

"I would never out you to the public, but in the case of Victor . . ." I set my water on the desk. "He deserves to know he's been loved this whole time. Tell him by Monday after the gazebo is gone, or I will. He deserves that much."

"I will not risk his health and security by telling him."

I thought of the framed gazebo picture in Victor's office. Right on his bookshelf in easy view from his desk. "Why do you want to take it down?"

"Because every time I see it, I remember."

I stood. "Others love looking at it to remember." I looked at the box under his hand. "Victor will want those letters."

WE EXITED Gable Green's mansion offices and two women were taking a smoke break on the ramp.

"Out of the way, please," I said, storming down first, clearing the path.

Hunter rolled after me. "Hold on, Marc. What's up?"

"I cannot believe this."

"Okay, you sound pissed."

I threw my hands up in exasperation. "Of course I'm pissed."

"Why?"

I whirled around, facing him. We were halfway down the path, surrounded by manicured grass and all those damn scampering squirrels. "On missions, when I make a grave mistake, you always sweep in and save the day."

"I do, don't I?"

"Yes, and I almost always appreciate it."

Hunter dimpled, deep.

I scowled. "Why didn't you stop me? Why didn't you shut me up and take his offer?"

Hunter scooted closer, tugged me onto his lap, and nipped a kiss on my jaw.

"I'm still pissed," I grumbled.

He rolled us toward his van. "Maybe I didn't think you needed rescuing?"

"But your gazebo. I just lost it."

"No, we lost K's support, we've still got moves."

"Like what?"

"We can chain ourselves to the pillars."

I snorted and kissed him back. "Don't think I won't."

In the van, I rubbed my hands over my knees. "How do we feel about making Victor a quick visit?"

"Thought you were giving Kyle time until Monday?"

I shrugged insolently. "I want to invite him to the goodbye-gazebo party."

His eyes twinkled. "There's a goodbye-gazebo party?"

"I'm thinking Monday morning around eleven?"

"What makes you think Victor will come?"

The photo of the gazebo in his room indicated it held sentimental value for him. Besides, if he knew what was really at stake . . . "What makes you think he won't?"

Hunter hummed. "If it were me . . . I'd come." Sunlight glittered over his lashes. "Do you have a date to take to this party?"

I whispered at his earlobe. "I sure do, and he's got some questions to ask me once the gazebo is saved."

Hunter side-eyed me. "You have nothing to prove."

The fuck I didn't. "Get driving."

"LIAM AND QUINN are coming over for pizza tonight," Hunter said after a brief visit to Victor, who'd paled at the idea of Monday's demolition.

We waited in line at an intersection. Left led back to my place. Right, his.

I rubbed my knees. "Will there be Supreme?"

"So you'll come?"

"If the invitation is extended to me."

"Consider it always extended to you. Just . . . it'll only be us four."

Quinn, Hunter, Liam, and me.

I nodded, properly exfoliating my palms. "Sure. Great. Bring on the BFFs."

The BFFs showed up at eight with pizzas. We ate, crowded

around the table, Hunter entertaining us with underdog sports tales. He spoke with his usual confident charisma, but at the edges, it sounded forced, like he needed for us all to get along.

I scooted into the kitchen for a refill of water, downed it, and startled Hunter with a wet kiss to his neck. He slapped the damp spot, grinning. Directly across from me, Quinn smirked at his slice of pizza. "Why call your thing a goodbye party and not a rally?"

"Mostly because more people might come."

"Ha." His gaze swung from Hunter to me. "I hope it . . . ends well."

Hunter cleared his throat. "How's teaching self-defense classes without my sis?"

"When is my darling Shannon getting back?"

"Next semester." Hunter segued into updates about Shannon's exchange, and Liam and I went for the last piece of Supreme.

"Oh," he said.

"No, you take it," I urged.

"You were angling for it."

"There are other slices."

"None as good as Supreme."

"Amen to that."

I withdrew my hand from the box, hoping he'd take the slice. "I see you also avoided the pizza with pineapple."

"It makes the base soggy."

"Exactly."

"And it has a numbing aftertaste."

"Right!"

Liam inclined his head and scooped up the last piece of Supreme. "This is strange."

"The pizza?"

"Us four. Hanging out so often."

Quinn seemed to have read between the lines, but I wasn't sure Liam had. "I hope you can get used to it."

"Used to it?" He paled, glancing at Hunter, who was scoffing at something Quinn said. "Are you two serious?"

I rubbed my nape. "Hey, do you want to walk to the store and pick up a bottle of wine with me?"

"Wine?"

"We may both need it after what I tell you."

Liam eyed me warily and stood. "I'm listening."

We left Hunter and Quinn and strode to a local liquor store. The place was quiet and every step sounded loud.

"White wine or red?"

"I don't drink often."

I nodded. "Oh, sure. We can grab something non-alcoholic, too . . ."

Liam rolled his shoulders. "I'll take a sip of red?"

We arrowed for the red section.

I picked a wine off the shelf, then set it back. "I make you uncomfortable."

"You used to. Now you make me wary . . . and curious." Liam scanned bottles. "What do you want to tell me?"

"So, it's about last year."

"Last year?"

"With how I . . . with how cruelly I treated you."

Liam shoved his glasses up. "Yes, I recall. What do you have to say about it?"

"I was an ass. An idiot of epic proportions. Every time I snickered, or joked, or made fun of you having no friends. Every pissed off moment I had when you landed the party page. Every—"

"That's much less vague," Liam said quickly, clicking the pen he always carried in his pocket. "You can stop the list now."

I cleared my throat. "Right. So, the thing is, I'm really, really sorry."

"Can you fast forward to the part about you and Hunter being serious?"

My stomach plummeted. I probably deserved that brush-off. "I know you think that he deserves better."

Liam frowned.

I hurried on. "I know I agreed."

"But?" he prompted.

"What we have is not meaningless. We are not just hanging out. We are getting to know one another. There are feelings. There are hearts on the line. Everything is at stake here."

"You want to be his boyfriend?"

I held his gaze. "I want to be your friend."

"Why?"

"Because you mean a lot to him, and there will be a lot of parties where we will fight out who gets the last slice of Supreme." I smirked.

"I was too hasty in some of my comments. Hunter has been radiant since summer, and I don't have trouble putting two and two together."

I grinned, hard, and plucked the first red I touched off the shelf. "He makes me glow too."

"Yes," Liam said as we lined up to pay, "he's turned you into a right sap."

I STAYED a right sap all weekend. The majority of it in Hunter's arms.

At least until Sunday, when he kicked me out. I'd "had enough space," and "needed to sort out my relationships."

Damn him for being reasonable. For being right.

So Sunday afternoon, I traipsed home in borrowed underwear.

I breathed in the familiar scent of leather and carpet, and followed the distant sound of music to the living room. Perched on the couch, Jason watched TV.

He spotted me and grabbed the remote.

"Freeze right where you are," I said. "Lay the remote down."

He held it steady. "This doesn't need to stay on."

"Oh, it most absolutely does."

Jason's brow quirked suspiciously. "Men in tights have never been your thing."

"Au contraire. Have you seen *Batman*? I've never had so much fun staring at spandex."

Jason dropped the remote.

"Cool," I said. "Where's Uncle Ben?"

"You missed your shopping date with him yesterday. He headed out for groceries."

Oh, shit. Had he waited all day for me to show up? He should've messaged me and scolded my ass. Was he giving me space to see if I'd turn up on my own?

A wave of regret funneled through me and I grabbed my phone and sent him an apology. Definitely better done in person, but I couldn't wait that long.

I edged into the living room. "What are you watching?"

Jason eyed me. "What are you doing, Marc?"

I slung myself into the free spot next to him. "It's been a big week for me. Big couple of weeks, actually, and I'm really tired. TV is exactly what I want right now."

Jason hummed. "Okay."

We sat side by side for half an hour, Jason explaining at regular intervals that the judges wanted artistry, flexibility, hip alignment . . .

He studied me. "Are you sure you want to watch this?"

"Sure." I rubbed my nape.

"You don't look so sure."

"That has nothing to do with ballet." I darted my gaze back to the TV screen. "I was a shit to you when I moved in with Uncle Ben."

He absorbed that and nodded. "To be fair, you were a shit to everyone. I wasn't special."

"Yeah. Did Uncle Ben tell you that?"

"Anyone could see it."

"I am sorry, Jason."

Jason rubbed my shoulder and squeezed comfortingly. "You were grieving."

"No excuse to be an asshole."

"True." He muted the TV. The quiet ratcheted my heartbeat. "I want to stay."

I waved my hand around. "There's certainly room for it. More soon, I hope."

"Your uncle doesn't want me to give up my job."

I smiled softly. "God, he's a good man."

Jason's eyes welled. "All this time and he never slept with anyone, being okay if I did . . . and the secret, Marc?" He blinked hard. "Neither did I."

My stomach did a happy little pirouette. "You've told him this?"

"I keep working up the guts."

"Hiding the truth won't land you the love you're looking for."

"I want him to admit he wants me here forever."

"Jason?"

"Yeah?"

"You're the only one in his world who calls him Harry."

Jason slammed his eyes shut and it was my turn to pat his shoulder. I stood. "Do you want a coke?"

His throat bulged with a swallow. "Zero, please."

I stepped into the hallway, and smacked into Uncle Ben near the door, staring at his feet. Behind him, shopping bags sat in the entranceway. How long had he been there?

One step, and he engulfed me in the tightest hug of my life.

"Um, okay," I whispered.

Five, six, seven seconds, he held me, wiry beard pressing at my throat. He pulled back and admired my face and kissed my forehead with a firm smack.

He let me go, straightened his posture, and walked into the living room. I waited, listening, much like Uncle Ben must have.

"Harry," Jason said, startled, and I imagined him lurching to his feet.

Uncle Ben's deep, gravelly voice cinched with sincerity. "I want you here forever."

CHAPTER SIXTEEN

"You don't have to do that."

Hunter looked over the orange he was peeling. "Do what?"

"Stop eating to make me breakfast."

"Sure I do," he said, continuing to peel the orange. "Or you'll eat all of mine."

"It is a really good fruit salad."

"Yes. And by all means, leave the apple."

"The pears, orange, and mango are yummier."

"An apple a day keeps the doctor away. So does this green smoothie." He pushed his glass toward me like he was serious.

I hastily plucked an apple out of his bowl and popped it into my mouth.

He laughed. "We're doomed already." Orange peel dropped to the wooden board and he growled at me. "You couldn't have told me that before I started peeling?"

"You underestimate how much I'm digging this fruit salad."

"Did you not eat before you came here?"

"Nope."

"Why not?"

"Oh, you know, I didn't want to wait a second longer to bug you." I flushed.

"Really," Hunter mused.

"I'm weirdly nervous. Neither of us knows what will happen today. I know we've done everything possible to save the gazebo, but . . . what if this truly is goodbye?"

"Then maybe," Hunter said, voice cracking, "it's told one last story."

I gripped his bowl as soft, sweeping shivers unsteadied me. Hunter's phone shrilled.

He raised orange sticky hands and I accepted the call from his mom. "Hey, Mrs. Hunter."

"Oh, Marc. I wasn't expecting you to answer." Her knowing smile brightened the screen. "We've arrived in Pittsburgh."

I cast Hunter a confused look. "This will be a day to remember. Here's your son."

Hunter blazed as he said hello. "Yeah, I'm okay."

"Just okay?" she hummed.

I plucked an orange from the bowl and enjoyed watching Hunter fluster. "Good. Real good. Um, so we'll meet you at the gazebo? Do lunch after?"

"Yes. Thank you for sending the draft of Marc's article, tell him we loved it."

He glanced over at me and I grinned.

"He heard you, mom."

"You two are . . . friendly."

"Yep. He came around for breakfast. Look, can we catch up later?"

"Of course, dear."

"Okay, bye." He hung up. "I forgot to mention they wanted to come to the gazebo-goodbye party."

"Definitely forgot that tidbit." I plucked out another apple. "Just came around for breakfast?"

"It's true."

"So you didn't hear the emphasis that suggested she thinks we're more?"

"I ignored it."

"Even though more is happening."

"I know, but . . ." Uncertainty and hope rimmed his eyes. He spoke quietly. "After today, right? After you announce what we are."

He swallowed and held his chin high. He knew what we were, yet that didn't change his need to hear it. To be certain, absolutely. "Hunter—"

The doorbell buzzed.

Liam and Quinn were at the door, Quinn grinning, Liam handsomely expressionless, each toting two coffees.

Liam handed me one of his, and Quinn tromped into the house calling after Hunter.

"Are you ready to go?" Liam asked.

"We were eating breakfast." I checked the time and swore. Damn time flew with Hunter. "Yeah, we're ready."

Liam wavered. "Should we meet you there?"

I heard Quinn's thumping steps and Hunter's wheels behind me. I jumped into my sneakers. "We're coming."

Liam led the way outside. "Please tell me we're walking."

Hunter rolled after him, ahead of Quinn and me, camera bag swinging from his chair. "Was that a dig at my driving?"

I snorted. "I hope so."

Liam smiled at me. "It most certainly was."

Quinn and I laughed until Hunter silenced us with a death glare.

"Don't be too upset, honey," I cooed. "You can laugh at me panting up the zigzag path."

"THIS IS A BARE-BONES PARTY," Liam said when we arrived on site to dewy grass, barren of life.

I leaned against him as we both stared at the turret-shaped roof, glittering with frost. "A few more people will turn up."

At least, I sincerely hoped.

Quinn glanced at our point of contact and suddenly found the roses fascinating, and in fact, Liam should definitely come check them out with him.

Hunter laughed and rubbed the back of my thigh. Could he feel my thrumming anxiety?

I folded my arms tight under my armpits. Would this be the gazebo's last day? All those inscribed names and padlocks—would those lovers be doomed?

I concentrated on the comforting warmth of Hunter's hand.

"Come," I murmured, curving around the gazebo. At the arch window where Hunter's parents had carved their names, roses pushed against us from either side. I pulled out the army knife I'd been carrying all morning.

"What's this?" Hunter said, gravelly.

"You know what this is."

Hunter eyed the knife. "It's only been a few weeks."

Plus an entire summer, but that didn't matter. "This is our tuna sandwich, Hunter."

I pressed the tip of the knife against the wood. It immediately shut down on my finger. "Motherfucker!"

Hunter warred between concern and laughter, opting for laughter.

I laughed too, sucked on the small cut, and handed the army knife to Hunter. "You have it. So much for being romantic."

Hunter chiseled our names into the wood a few inches below his parents. Proudly staring at it, he fondled the back of my thigh again, and warmth oozed through my bones. I examined his defined features—the pouty bottom lip, the hard line of his nose, the straight lashes. I breathed in cool air and exhaled a faint cloud toward him.

Somewhere in the distance Liam and Quinn were murmuring.

Hunter withdrew his camera and took a shot of our names, then snuck a candid shot of me watching him.

"Hannah's here. With Victor."

I shot my head around. Victor, holding his cane and a contemplative look, waltzed toward the ramp like he was breathing in the past. They acknowledged us with a wave, but before we could head over, Mary called from the top of the path, waving and yoo-hooing us, arm hooked around Dan's.

"Hey, Mom. Dad," Hunter greeted, and we halted before them.

Two sets of humored eyes soaked me in—barely a nod to Hunter. "Marc. Lovely to meet you in person."

Hunter cleared his throat. "Was it a good flight?"

"Good, yes." Dan said distractedly. His eyes jumped from ecstatic to telling me if I hurt Hunter, I would have him to reckon with. I nodded to Dan's silent warning. "We're glad we could come support you."

"Thank you," I croaked.

"Mom—" Hunter said.

She kissed her son's cheek. "What have we missed?" She waved a hand around us and the gazebo.

"You're just in time, the bulldozer is driving up now," Hunter said, gesturing behind them. "You haven't missed anything."

"Well, one thing," I said, stepping behind Hunter and resting my hands on his shoulders.

Hunter flexed under me and cocked his head back, like he wasn't sure if I was saying what I was most definitely saying.

I grinned down at him. "Marc?" he asked softly.

"The thing is, Hunter," I whispered, in full view of his parents. "I don't want to live regretting things anymore."

I kissed him softly, just the touch of my lips against his, and electricity consumed me. I breathed it in for a beat, and reluctantly drew back, winking at his beaming parents. "I didn't just come around for breakfast," I said. "I came around to be with my boyfriend."

I was engulfed in a Dan-and-Mary shaped hug. Hunter laughed. "Don't smother him."

"It's okay," I said, words muffled in Mary's scarf. "I like it."

When they released me, Hunter gave his parents a warning stare and lured me to our quiet spot between the roses.

"Are you frisky?" I asked. "I'm all good for some public fun, but your parents catching us . . ."

Hunter leveled me a quit-it look, and I quit. His stare softened, intensified, and my heart banged about in my chest.

"You don't want to live with regrets anymore?" he murmured.

I swallowed. "I've been doing it too long already. If I didn't kiss you, if I didn't call you my boyfriend in front of your parents, if I didn't let you know that I'm yours, gazebo or not, I'd regret it forever."

Hunter knotted our fingers together, holding on tight like a promise. I closed my eyes like the sap I was under it all, letting the momentous feeling glow through me.

A kiss brushed over my knuckles. Sweet, simple, perfect.

Bit by bit, a few dozen people joined us at Lover's Loop. Students I'd never seen before—except, was that Tyler behind that broad jock?

"I mentioned it in my last *Scribe* article," I said to Hunter, perplexed, amazed. "But I didn't think people would come."

The crowd buffered the gazebo from the bulldozer and its workers.

I climbed the gazebo window and grinned over a sea of heads when I caught Uncle Ben and Jason, melting into the crowd, hand in hand.

Uncle Ben flashed me a thumbs up, and Jason smiled, relaxed, happy. Every move they made would now be made together.

Hannah tapped my shoulder and I jumped off the window. Beside her, Victor scanned the crowd in much the same way Kyle Gable Green had during his speech at the alumni party—and of course, Kyle had been hoping to see Victor.

Would Victor see Kyle?

"Would you answer a few questions?" Hannah asked me a dozen interview questions and Hunter promised he'd document with pictures of the event as it unfolded.

More students joined the goodbye party, along with Mr. Wyatt, the senior adviser in charge.

I faced his frustration.

"Look, even though I'm touched by your turnout and initiative, property services do not have the budget to make repairs. For the safety of everyone, we need to tear the gazebo down."

I blew the bangs out of my eyes. "What are you looking at for repairs? A couple grand?" I walked away, tossing over my shoulder, "We'll score that money."

Hunter hummed as he rolled beside me. "How are we getting a couple thousand dollars?"

I scrubbed my face. "Somehow."

The gazebo stood proudly amid the chaos. Pretty. Romantic. Victor and Hannah picturesque in the arch.

Inspiration warmed me like the sunshine. I eyed Hunter. "We're, uh, good looking guys."

He looked perplexed.

"We can position ourselves under the gazebo arch. It'd make a nice kissing booth."

Hunter halted abruptly and I turned to face him.

"You want to sell kisses?" he said.

"Either that, or we offer them a show. But I don't think the university would approve. We also might get arrested."

Hunter puffed out his chest before he sighed. "Bring on the kisses."

"Oh, I have a better idea." I smirked when I saw Kyle approach through the thick crowd.

I raced to Victor. "Will you offer up kisses for money to save the gazebo?"

Victor's spirited, disbelieving laugh carried. "No one wants to kiss an old man."

"Quick," Hunter said under his tongue. "He's coming."

"I'll give you ten bucks to kiss you."

"You're crazy."

I fished out ten from my wallet and handed it to Hannah. "You take care of monies."

I cupped Victor's soft cheeks, and he laughed again. "Ten dollars won't save the gazebo, and no one else will pay to kiss me."

"Out of the way." Kyle growled, stalking up the ramp. I pretended I didn't hear him, and leaned closer to Victor, feeling the drag of his shocked inhale. "Kyle?" he whispered.

"Stop, I beg you." Kyle's voice was raw with emotion.

I pivoted around as if startled. Maybe bullshitting had no place masking real emotions, but there were times where it did the job. Like now. "But we're raising money for repairs to save the gazebo—"

"Step aside."

I stepped aside, and Kyle halted before Victor.

They stared at each other like the two long lost lovers they were. Sunlight streamed over them in thick, sparkling rays. Their gazes held a million unspoken words, and tension ratcheted. Next came The Lean.

Cliché.

I loved it.

Abruptly, Kyle turned to face the murmuring crowd and the bulldozer men huddled at the street.

"We will not be needing your services today. I'll see that you are paid and that there are funds for repairs."

A simple statement, yet the crowd's response was a boom of a thousand cymbals.

Uncle Ben whooped loudly, and K swiveled toward Hunter and me. "Thank goodness for meddling kids?" He blew out a breath and murmured, "I took your advice. Thank you for persuading me." He faced Victor. Their gazes clashed with palpable energy and K resumed his lean, smiling softly, hopefully. His hand shook as he reached up and smoothed it over Victor's shoulder, curving around his nape.

Hunter clasped the back of my thigh as if he, like me, was tense with anticipation. I threaded my fingers between his and our pressure tightened as Kyle pulled Victor close. Almost a kiss, but not quite. "May I?"

I swallowed hard as I watched Victor's gaze dazzle in surprise and wonder.

Victor's breath hiccupped. "I hoped you'd come today. Thank you for sending your letters."

"You read them?"

"Over and over."

Kyle's voice broke, "I missed you, Victor."

Wrinkles around Victor's eyes deepened into a startling smile, full of life. Love. "How much?"

Kyle smiled into a kiss.

My heart soared all the way through it and during the jubilant celebration afterward.

Everywhere, people were laughing, overjoyed. Hunter's parents braved the inside of the gazebo; Jason grabbed a handful of Uncle Ben's shirt and hauled him into a smooch; Hannah busily wrote notes. Liam tucked against Quinn's chest, a genuine smile on his face . . .

Hunter snagged me onto his lap in the shadows of roses. "Look at you, so cocky."

"Yep." I buckled out a laugh. Would I ever get used to the tickling lightness inside?

"What's that for?"

"Nothing much. This must have been an excellent morning for you."

He quirked a questioning brow.

I stage-whispered, "There was so much cheese."

Hunter tipped my forehead to his. "And there was my knight in shining armor."

I snorted, then kissed the fuck out of him.

CHAPTER SEVENTEEN

To go to bed or not to?

Shivers from Hunter's sneaky looks shot through my chest to my toes.

It'd been nearly six months since saving the gazebo. Six months basking in the glow of being Hunter's boyfriend. Six months living with him, studying together for exams, and working as a bartender at Phoenix for some extra cash.

Should I shut my laptop and jump him, or pretend his sexy looks weren't distracting me?

I bit my bottom lip and concentrated on moving my knight into the witch's cottage. AfteriMage, formerly DaMage, followed me and was quick to start plucking herbs and concocting a spell to ward off the demons on our tail.

I jumped into the chat box.

Me: Are you doing that on purpose?

AfteriMage: Preparing to save your ass?

Me: Scoping it out like you want to ravage it.

Hunter barked out a laugh from his end of the couch.

AfteriMage: Do you think I have a chance?

Me: You know you do.

AfteriMage: But you want me to blast these last demons away first.

Me: You're so good at it.

AfteriMage: You're not so bad yourself, Marc.

Even though I was one hundred percent open with Hunter, I still felt the urge to hide my flushing cheeks. "It's bubbling up, Hunter, I'm about to say it. For the third time today."

"Say what?" he goaded.

I narrowed my eyes, refusing to give in just yet. "Not now. Your geek-God ass has magic to make."

Hunter bowed his head toward his computer, smirking.

I added, "But when you're done, I'll whisper it to you."

Like I'd done the first time, the night after we'd saved the gazebo . . .

We'd slid into Hunter's freshly changed bedsheets, light casting a bright glow. We wrestled for being on top, Hunter muscling me to the bed, both of us laughing, high and uncontrolled. Hunter's tattooed arms flexed, hummingbirds fluttering like I was fluttering inside. Light and filled with bright relief and happiness. I grabbed a pillow and yelled into it.

Hunter drew it away.

"I could fucking live off your laugh." I snatched him into a kiss, and he indulged.

He drew back staring at me, laughter morphing into something softer, deeper, far more intense.

His skin pressed against mine; I ran my hands over his back, cursing how beautiful he was. So much so that I had to leave a mark. On his neck, his shoulder, his nipple.

Hunter let out frustrated whimpers and commanded me to wriggle back up.

"Why?" I said, face to face again, grinning.

He pressed a soft kiss against the corner of my mouth. "I can't get enough of this."

I soaked in the miraculous feeling of his weight against me, cupped the back of his neck and drew him closer. His earlobe tickled my lip, and my breath crackled. "I love you."

Hunter settled his laptop into his wheelchair, startling me to the present. "I magicked away the demons, while you . . . what were you daydreaming about?"

I smiled fondly at him. "The first time I said those words."

Hunter beckoned for my laptop and set it aside.

He drummed the back of the couch. "You gonna tell me them again or what?"

I lunged into his arms and kissed all the smiles out of him. I was gonna tell him again, all right. Tonight, and every night.

I smiled against his temple, and he beat me to it. "I love you, too, Marc."

~The End~

ACKNOWLEDGMENTS

I couldn't have written this book without the rock-solid support of my hubby. You are an amazing dad, and I love navigating this parental adventure with you. As always, you are my inspiration for writing romance. You set a high bar, love.

A huge thank you to Sunne without whom this story would not exist. Thank you for loving Liam Davis & The Raven and for plotting Marc Jillson's story arc with me. That week with you in Switzerland was incredible!

Vir and Heather. Thank you for all your tremendous guidance to help shape this story—it was a pleasure to work with you.

Thank you to Rebecca for sensitivity reading and giving me your valuable feedback.

Cheers to HJS Editing for all the fantastic edits and the fast turn-around. And thank you to Lynda Lamb at *Refinery* for proofreading, and Todd, Alex, Neta for proofing the story, and Vicki for being a wonderful final eyes reader.

Lastly, big thank you to Natasha for designing the cover. I love how well you captured Hunter's spirit.

ANYTA SUNDAY

Heart-stopping slow burn

A bit about me: I'm a big, BIG fan of slow-burn romances. I love to read and write stories with characters who slowly fall in love.

Some of my favorite tropes to read and write are: Enemies to Lovers, Friends to Lovers, Clueless Guys, Bisexual, Pansexual, Demisexual, Oblivious MCs, Everyone (Else) Can See It, Slow Burn, Love Has No Boundaries.

I write a variety of stories, Contemporary MM Romances with a good dollop of angst, Contemporary lighthearted MM Romances, and even a splash of fantasy.
My books have been translated into German, Italian, French, Spanish, and Thai.

Contact: http://www.anytasunday.com/about-anyta/
Sign up for Anyta's newsletter and receive a free e-book:
http://www.anytasunday.com/newsletter-free-e-book/